BU

"Brawley's terrain gazes...read...non-stop, pages in a flash. The Alaska environment...large after all though the artistry...vivid descriptions...who would...me feel as though I were there. The story had me from the beginning, start—wilderness, wildlife, and dangers throw man on...rediscovery...and a unlikely couple who have a smoldering dread...of and I couldn't put it down—highly recommended."

—J. DERRICK AUTHOR

Burning Secrets is a romance with a dangerous ride. I loved the one most beautiful...feld like the action was more intense and easy. I love the whole series...for just in my opinion this book be...more in the subject of your car, nail biting, heart-stopping, adventure and action. This is well worth $5.72 to buy.

—DANA GOODLAND

"I love unique...the unique plot, the characters...he faith thread and care...of and able to connect me emotionally to the characters. Three—worth LERHRN...Is there books such entertaining and pace."

—THE LITERATE FRIEND SARK GOODREADS

BURNING
SECRETS

BURNING SECRETS

SUSAN MAY WARREN

sunrise
PUBLISHING

Burning Secrets
Chasing Fire: Alaska, Book 4

Copyright © 2025 Sunrise Media Group LLC
Print ISBN: 978-1-966463-00-9

This book is a work of fiction. Names, characters, places, and incidents are either products of the author's imagination or used fictitiously. Any similarity to actual people, organizations, and/or events is purely coincidental. All Scripture quotations, unless otherwise indicated, are taken from the The ESV® Bible (The Holy Bible, English Standard Version®), © 2001 by Crossway, a publishing ministry of Good News Publishers. Used by permission. All rights reserved.

For more information about Susan May Warren, please access the author's website at www.susanmaywarren.com.

Published in the United States of America.

Cover Design: Sunrise Media Group LLC

· CHASING FIRE ALASKA ·

To my amazing fans.
I'm so grateful for you!

Soli Deo Gloria

ONE

NORMAL PEOPLE, ON THEIR DAY OFF, might go into town, grab a pizza, a chocolate shake, maybe hang out with the other smoke-jumpers.

But apparently, she wasn't normal.

Although, JoJo might have thought to take her tracker ring with her so that when she was mauled and left for dead in the high Alaskan woods, someone might find her carcass and inform her poor mother.

After five years watching her daughter jump out of airplanes into the mouth of the dragon, her worst fears would come true on a bright, sunny day in a clump of wild blueberry bushes.

JoJo held her breath, didn't move as the grizzly,

13

his feral scent souring the air, snuffled through the thick bushes, hunting for lunch. He'd come up on her like smoke, as if from nowhere, just the redolence of him a hint of trouble as she'd trained her binoculars some forty yards ahead to a secluded burrow near the river.

Please, let the pups still be alive.

The river—just a meandering tributary off the main channel of the Copper River that ran from the lumbering Denali massif—carved out caves and indentations as it cut south through tundra and alpine woods and splashed over rocky cliffs. She would never have located Cleo and her mate, Brutus, if it weren't for the tracking collars the ADF&G had placed on the wolves two years ago.

And she owed wolf researcher and her mentor, Peyton Samson, the thanks for allowing her to observe the mating pair and their pups for her research paper.

Finally put her master's degree to bed.

More snuffing, and the mnemonic from her mother trickled through her head. *If it's black, fight back. If it's brown, lay down.*

As in play dead.

She glanced over, spotted the grizzly scruff of its neck in her peripheral vision, maybe twenty yards away, and slowly lowered herself to the stony earth, pulling her hood up, her body in the fetal position.

Her heartbeat rushed in her ears, nearly deafening.

Breathe. Don't move.

And for some reason, Jade Ransom, her jump boss, entered her head. *Where do you go on your days off? You're always disappearing.*

Yeah, maybe she shouldn't be quite so private. It wasn't like she was breaking any laws. She just preferred the quiet, the aloneness. No one to get in her way.

No one to break her heart. The breath of the Alaska air, just her and the wilderness.

Maybe she was like her father in that way. She hoped so.

Sticks broke, more rustling. Snuffing.

Her hand trekked down her leg to her bear spray in her thigh holster. Who knew if it might actually repel the grizzly? Better to hide. But should the animal—

Barking. Then a growl and more barking, and she wanted to push herself up, to see if—

Yes, it sounded like Brutus. Maybe protecting his den.

Weird that Cleo wasn't with him, but JoJo

15

hadn't seen the pups, so maybe Cleo was out hunting. Still, alone? That didn't feel right.

Although, recently, a lot didn't feel right. Like her team's recent run-in with some crazy Alaskan militia group who'd tried to kill them.

And never mind the *plane crash* that they'd narrowly escaped. Then, while they'd hiked back to civilization, her other team members had been chased down, met a rogue cult, found dead salmon in a river, found a homesteader lady in the woods who'd been drugged, and one of the team had been *kidnapped*.

She hadn't been sad they'd left without her on that spur-of-the-moment trip. Still, it felt like the entire world had gone crazy up here in the land of the never-ending sun.

The grizzly growled, turning, breaking branches, trampling the bushes.

She pushed herself up. All around her on the hillside, blueberry bushes poked up around boulders. The hill pitched down to a ten-foot drop into a rocky riverbed and its glistening river in the valley below.

Brutus paced on a large flat-topped rock, his fur ruffed, barking, foam at his mouth. The grizzly lumbered nearby, nearly ignoring him as he foraged.

Where was his pack? She lifted her glasses, scanned the area. Brutus and Cleo had returned to the den they'd used last year. The pack usually congregated in and around the craggy shoreline. This year, however, they seemed more scattered, the pack thinner.

He wouldn't take on a bear without the pack. Not unless . . .

He hadn't gotten ousted as alpha, had he? She searched his body for wounds, evidence of a fight.

Brutus rushed at the bear, who turned, swatted. Brutus jerked away, snarling, barking.

The bear landed on all fours, growled, and then shook his head side to side. Agitated. Nervous.

Watch out, Brutus. The grizzly huffed, stomped, but Brutus stood his ground, snapping, growling, barking.

She tucked away her bear spray, picked up her phone. Snapped a picture.

And then, just like that, the bear moved off, turning, lumbering away.

Brutus climbed the flat stone, barking after it. Still growling.

She stood, took another picture of the wolf, deep-gray hair along its body, white tufted hair between his legs and along his snout, dark black eyes, a bushy light-gray tail, a ring of black at the end.

A beautiful alpha male. And maybe he'd just saved her life.

And this, right here, was why she'd come to Alaska. Sure, she'd joined the Midnight Sun fire crew, but that had simply landed her on the map in the right place. Given her a reason to show up at the Forest Service office in search of Professor Samson, who'd guest taught for a week at Montana State University in Bozeman.

Right then, JoJo had known what she wanted to do with her life.

Study these animals, discover what made them fierce and brave and enabled them to thrive in the harsh Alaskan frontier.

Maybe figure out how to do the same.

Brutus turned and looked at her, straight on. The breeze picked up, rustled the brush, combed through his hair.

He didn't seem displaced from leadership.

And then he growled. A low, lethal warning.

Oh. She pocketed her phone. Kept eye contact. "No need for that, Brute." *Get bigger.* She spotted a rock, climbed on it. Raised her arms.

His growl deepened, and he lowered his head.

"I'm not the bad guy!" She clapped her hands.

"Go away!" She grabbed her whistle, blew it, piercing, bright, shrill.

He raised his lips in a snarl.

What was his deal? She'd gotten too close once, and he'd emerged from the den, but she'd simply backed away, and he'd let her go.

"I'm not going to hurt your pups, Brute." She clapped her hands, then unzipped her jacket and held it open. "Go away!"

He took a step toward her, and she reached for her bear spray. "Don't make me use this—"

The wolf launched at her.

She screamed, stumbled back, slipped and slammed into the bramble, bounced off, hit the rocky edge with her hip.

Pain exploded through her body, but she rolled, found the spray. Screamed.

Brutus appeared above her, snarling, barking, nipping.

She deployed the spray as Brutus leaped at her. The spray burned him in the face, and he yelped.

She scrambled for footing. Stood.

He shook off the chemicals and rounded on her, furious.

"Brutus—" She scrambled back. "Don't—"

She sprayed again—nothing. Empty. She took

another step back, threw the can at him, and reached for her gun.

Shoulder holster, and she hated to go for the .44, but she didn't want to be torn limb from limb either. She held it out, took off the safety. "Please, go!" She shouted it, hoping the noise might deter him.

He didn't look right. Pacing, his eyes glossy, foam at his mouth—rabies?

She took another step back and rocks fell. She glanced back—

Brutus launched at her.

She turned, squeezed off a shot, and the recoil jerked her back.

Yelping, she took her eyes off Brutus as she windmilled her arms for purchase, but the momentum yanked her back, and she stumbled into air, the cliff dropping from behind her—

Falling.

She screamed and landed with a hard, brutal *whuff*, ten feet below, her breath jerking out of her body.

Writhing for air, her bones shuddering, everything inside her on fire.

A growl above her, and as she fought to breathe, Brutus appeared over her on the rock above.

She got her hands up just as he leaped.

Breathe! She rolled, waiting for him to land, but a shot broke the air.

Crisp and echoing across the mountainscape.

Brutus dropped next to her on the rocky ground, gone.

She lay breathing, over and over, shaking.

Brutus's glassy eyes stared at her, the life winked out, blood puddling the ground under him.

And all she could do was curl into a ball, hands over her head, and weep.

Please, let him not have killed her.

Crew lowered his Winchester, his body shaking. Picked up his monocular. She lay on the ground, unmoving, the wolf next to her.

He wasn't the best shot, and frankly, he'd end up back in jail if anyone found him in possession of a gun.

But from his vantage point, some four hundred yards away atop a nearby rise that overlooked the Copper River spring, it clearly looked like the wolf had intended on having the woman for dinner.

He'd had no choice—the story of his life, the conundrum driving every decision for the past few weeks since the sister of his cohort Tristan had stumbled onto the Sons of Revolution base camp.

And then the world had just exploded. Literally. The camp had gone up in a ball of fire while Tristan and Jamie had escaped. And then he'd watched a plane of smokejumpers go down, and that had sat in his gut like ash until he'd found out no one had died.

Still, he hated this job.

"Crew—you still there?" The voice crackled in his earpiece, and he jerked, tearing his gaze off the downed woman.

Rio, on the other end of the sketchy transmission. And who knew how much his handler had heard of his report?

"Was that a gunshot? You okay?"

"Not me. Long story—" The phone line cut out, crackled. "Rio?"

Sheesh, the call cut off. Perfect. He worked out his earbud and pocketed it as he strode toward the four-wheeler. Wouldn't be long before Viper and Jer started asking about him, expecting him back from his perimeter sweep.

But he couldn't leave her down there.

From here, the rise fell in a not-so-gentle slope down to the valley floor, but he'd trekked up a deer trail on the backside of the hill, so maybe he could find a way down.

He raced the four-wheeler back to the trail, ducking against bramble and low-hanging, shaggy arms of pine and aspen trees. Emerging onto the valley floor, he turned and gunned the four-wheeler over mossy rocks, crushing magenta fireweed and tall blue lupine and violet wild irises, so much beauty in a brutal land.

The woman wore a blue jacket, hiking boots, and lay still, curled in a ball next to the wolf.

But his heart nearly stopped when she lifted her head. Sat up, staring hard at him.

Pretty. Brown hair, long and in a braid, wide hazel-green eyes, long lashes, a sweetheart face, and it hit him that he'd maybe seen her before.

Maybe around Copper Mountain, one of the many tourists.

He braked.

She lifted a gun.

What? He raised his arms. "Don't shoot."

Her grip shook, and tears glazed her eyes. Had she been crying? "Stay back!"

He eased off the four-wheeler. "Calm down—"

"Calm down? Did you shoot Brutus?"

Who? "Are you hurt?"

She stared at him, her hand still shaking, wiped the other hand across her cheek.

"So maybe put the gun down." He took a step toward her.

"Stay. Back!"

He stopped. Glanced at the mound of fur at her feet. "Listen. I'm sorry about the wolf. I thought he was going to attack you."

She drew in a breath, glanced at the wolf, nodded. "I don't know—he was acting . . . it's not normal."

Not—"What, you two have a long-standing friendship?"

Oops. He'd been kidding, but her gaze snapped up to his.

"Yes, as a matter of fact. I've been studying Brutus and his mate, Cleo, for the past month, watching their cubs, documenting their behavior. And yeah, Brutus has seen me before, but he's never attacked me." Her gun had lowered, her voice breaking. "Something was wrong."

His gaze stayed on the gun. "What kind of wrong?"

"He seemed unhinged, unafraid of me."

"Was he protecting his young?"

She had crouched beside the wolf, lifting his eyelids. "Yes. I don't know. Maybe."

He took another step toward her, the ground crunching beneath his hiking boot.

She looked up. "Stay."

He raised his hands again. "I'm not going to hurt you."

Her eyes narrowed and then glanced at the four-wheeler behind him, and something flashed in her eyes. Fear?

It occurred to him then how he looked—camo jacket, filthy hat over his dark hair, scruffy beard, canvas pants, a .308 Winchester strapped to his machine. The unofficial uniform of a Son of Revolution, and wasn't that nice?

Whatever respite he'd found on top of the hill, away from the darkness, settled right back into his soul, a deep ash that stained everything.

His voice softened. "I was just out checking traps."

Her mouth tightened. "And now I know you're lying, because there is no trapping season open in Alaska right now."

Oh.

Shoot.

He sighed, ran a hand across his chin. "Fine. I'm not out trapping. But I promise I mean you no harm."

"You shot at me!"

"I shot at the wolf. Trying to *kill you*."

She considered him a moment, then shoved her Magnum into her shoulder holster. "Fine. Prove it. Help me get Brutus on your four-wheeler and back to my truck."

He raised an eyebrow. "What?"

She'd started hiking toward the cliff, up the hill from where she'd fallen. "I need to get him to Copper Mountain so we can do an autopsy."

"I think I know how he died." He looked at the wolf. His shot had landed in his body—rib cage—left a bloody through-and-through. Blood caked his fur, puddled the ground, and an odor lifted. Gross.

"Don't be a jerk," she said, now from atop the cliff. She held a backpack. "Listen—okay, yes, he was . . ."

"Attacking you?"

"Acting deranged. Maybe rabies, so yes, thank you." She turned and headed back down the hill.

He crouched. The animal had blood in its teeth, foam at its lips. A feral odor lifted from its body.

Her boots crunched up to him. "Do you have a tarp or anything?"

He stood up. She wasn't tall—maybe five inches shorter than him—but she owned a presence about her that suggested she fancied herself in charge. Blood prickled along a scrape on her jaw. "You sure you're okay? That's not a short fall." He indicated the cliff. "Maybe you need to get checked out."

"I've had harder falls, believe me. Tarp?"

His eyes narrowed a moment, then he headed over to the four-wheeler and opened up the seat. Wire, ammo, knife, the radio to the compound—turned off—a fire-starting kit, a rope, and there, grimy and wadded on the bottom, an orange rain poncho. He pulled it out. Shook it open. "This could work."

"Thanks, MacGyver." She took it. "Help me roll this guy into it."

"Tell me again why we're bringing this show-and-tell to Copper Mountain?"

She'd crouched and spread the poncho out on the ground beside the wolf. He helped her and then took the animal's front legs as she took the back, and they rolled it onto the plastic.

"There's some rope too." He went to retrieve the rope and knife.

"I think he might have ingested something—a hallucinogenic or maybe eaten some poison." She wrapped the animal in the poncho, held the poncho shut as he secured it with the rope, making a sort of bundle.

Her words were a punch. Hallucinogenic? Oh no . . . He stared at the wolf, the darkness seeping into his bones, his breath. And then her other word hit him. *Ingested.* "As in he ate something?"

"Maybe. Take that end. Let's lift him."

He grabbed the animal and helped her lift him onto the back of the four-wheeler. Secured him with a couple bungie ropes, the math of her words freezing him through.

The food supply.

Oh no. But it made sense—

She'd stepped away from the four-wheeler, pulled out a monocular, and now scanned the riverbed.

"What are you looking for?"

"The pups. And his alpha female, Cleo." She sighed, turned. "You haven't seen anything . . . like dead salmon in the river, have you?"

He raised an eyebrow. "Why?"

And the answer, of course, was yes. Oh no, *yes*.

He wanted to hit something.

"Just . . . nothing." She frowned. Eyed his four-wheeler again, then looked at him, her jaw tight. And he didn't know why, but he had the strangest urge to raise his hands again.

Silence thrummed between them, back-dropped by the river rushing by, the hush lifting into the breeze.

"Who are you again?" she asked.

And for a second, he was back on the cliff, twenty minutes before he'd taken the shot, waiting for Rio to text him. Staring at the blue sky, the clouds congregating at the peak of the Denali massif. Surveying the vast green of the aspen and Sitka spruce, the craggy gray of the jutting mountains, the wildflower beauty of the valley. Even smelling the crisp, boreal-scented wind and hearing his own voice.

Lord, I need light. I need hope. I need answers. I need out.

And maybe that's why he looked at her, took a breath, and said the first true thing he'd said in over a year. "My name is Michael Crew Sterling. And I promise you, I'm one of the good guys." He stuck out his hand. "You can call me Crew."

She considered him a moment. A long, fragile moment where his hand sort of hung in the wind.

Then she sighed and took it. "I'm going to choose to trust you, Crew. Joann Butcher. My friends call me JoJo."

"Are we friends, then?"

29

Her mouth pinched. "As long as you don't try and kill me."

His mouth quirked. "Not real high standards, then. I think I have a real chance here."

She frowned, and then just like that, laughed. It emerged light and sweet and maybe a little short, but with it, light simply poured into his soul, swept out his breath.

He stared at her, nearly clutched his chest.

Yes, he wanted out, and now.

"Let's get going so I can get back and figure out if his pups are in trouble."

Oh.

He climbed onto the four-wheeler. Moved his foot so she could climb up behind him, her legs around his, her body against his back.

"Hang on," he said. "It's bumpy."

"I'm not going anywhere," she said, and gripped the side handles on the seat.

And as he pulled out across the bumpy terrain, all he could think was . . . I hope not.

TWO

SHE MIGHT BE HURT MORE THAN SHE let on. And the ride on the four-wheeler hadn't helped, bumping over rocks and tundra and forest and up jagged hills. By the time they'd gotten to the dirt road where she'd parked her truck, everything hurt.

Even her teeth.

She made the mistake of groaning as she got off the ATV and then nearly dropping her end of Brutus's carcass, which, of course, her hero had to grab to put into the truck.

She gripped the end of the tailgate and tried not to let her knees buckle.

Crew had taken one look at her, then grabbed her elbow and led her to the passenger door.

"What are you doing?"

31

For the first time, really, she noticed his eyes. Dark brown, with gold at the iris and the tiniest hint of concern in them.

Maybe not so tiny. "I'm driving you into Copper Mountain." He reached for the door handle.

She slammed her hand on it. "No. I can—"

"You're still shaking."

Oh.

"Get in. I can get a ride back to my ATV."

She frowned even as she let him open the door. "Really?"

"Please. You can't live in Alaska without friends." He then winked at her, and she had nothing for that.

He closed the tailgate, moved his ATV off the road, into the brush, hidden, and got into the driver's side.

She handed him the keys, leaned her head back.

And promptly fell asleep. Or would have if he hadn't jostled her awake.

"No sleeping."

She stared at him, wide-eyed, sitting up.

"You might have a concussion."

"For the love—I got up at three a.m. And it's now—"

"Six p.m. So yes, I get that, but you're still not sleeping. And why so early?"

She'd hiked in from the road, a couple miles to her lookout over the river, the spot a good ten miles north of Copper Mountain, and now she spotted civilization amid the deep green forest that hugged the road. Dirt roads led back from the main road north of town to quiet housing areas—log cabins and timber homes set upon the bustling Copper River. Now and again, a sign designating a road mark—Starr Lake and Mulligan Way and Bowie Road. He slowed as they came closer to town, passing the airfield with its multicolored Cessnas, De Havillands, and Cubs. A couple choppers also sat on the tarmac.

Her base also had an airfield, as did many private homes here in the bush. Truly the last frontier.

"Because it's my only free day, and I needed to get as much observation in as I could."

"Free day?"

"Day off. Head into the ranger's station. Hopefully Peyton is still around." She pointed down Main Street to the ranger's station at the end, just before the park and the river.

And across the street from Starlight Pizza. As if wishing, her stomach growled.

He glanced at her, a smile perking at his lips.

Probably she owed him a thank-you, because the longer they'd driven, the more she'd replayed Brutus's behavior.

And the louder the shot had echoed in her brain.

Brutus would have ripped out her throat. She saw it in her head, and the truth had fallen to her heart, her gut, her bones.

No wonder she was still shaking.

Crew pulled up to the ranger's station, a sort of cabin with a wide front porch, steps leading down to the street. He got out, stood on the sidewalk, glancing around as if looking for someone.

Interesting. But if he lived around here, probably he knew a few locals.

She came around the back of the truck. "Thanks—"

"You don't think I'm just going to leave you on the sidewalk with a dead wolf?" He raised an eyebrow.

Oh.

"Okay, um . . . well, let's leave him here, let Peyton take a look at him. She'll know what to do."

"Peyton?"

"She's the local wolf expert."

He followed her up the steps and inside.

Hank Billings, the ranger in charge, looked up from his office behind a wall of glass. She'd met him earlier this summer, back when she'd landed in Copper Mountain after her three-day drive north. Grimy, smelly, and tired, she'd felt like a stalker asking for Peyton.

Hank had sent her over to the Samson Bed and Breakfast, and there, she'd cleaned up, eaten a pile of sourdough pancakes, and met her mentor.

Now, Hank came out of his office. "Jo. What's up?"

"Peyton around?"

He glanced at her office. "She was. Not sure where she went—"

"I'm here."

The voice came from the door, where Peyton came in dressed in green canvas pants and a light-green shirt. "That a wolf in your truck, JoJo?"

"Brutus. He was shot."

Peyton wore her dark hair back under a yellow handkerchief, and her dark eyes glanced at Crew.

"He was attacking me."

Peyton cocked her head. "You get too close to the den?"

"No. I was forty yards away, easy. He came up behind me and—well, first he stood up to a grizzly, then he turned on me. He wasn't right,

Peyton. Something wasn't right. And Cleo and her pups aren't in the den."

Peyton gestured for them to follow and led them into her office, a tall standing desk against one wall, a map dotted with pushpins in different colors on the other. Gear on the floor—collars, tracking devices, backpacks.

"I have a team of interns showing up in a week, going to help me tag and collar the pups."

JoJo would like to be on that team. But they only did the work—they didn't stick around to observe. Besides, her fire team needed her, and frankly, that was in her blood too.

Peyton stepped up to her computer, opened a screen, and peered at the tracking on it. "Cleo's tracker is still active. And yes, it looks like they moved their den. She's localized in an area about a half mile south of the river den."

"Send me the pin and I'll take a look," JoJo said, stepping up behind her.

Peyton turned, her mouth a grim line. "She's without her alpha mate. That's going to be a problem. The pups are probably three months old, which means they still need her protection, and they might even be nursing, although they're probably eating solid food too. They might even be leaving the pack."

Jojo nodded. "And without the alpha there, they could be in trouble from an outsider who might want to come in and take over. He could kill the cubs, try and get Cleo to go into heat earlier to sire his own offspring."

Crew had walked to the board, studying it. Now he glanced at her, an eyebrow up.

"The pack has a pretty strong beta named Caesar. He might jump in as alpha," Peyton said. She turned back to her computer. Made a noise.

"What?" JoJo asked.

"Caesar and the others in the pack seem to have separated themselves from Cleo and the pups. They could just be hunting, but they've moved downstream, toward the main river."

She turned back to JoJo. "I'll keep an eye on the pack and Cleo and let you know what we find out from the autopsy."

"Thanks."

"I'll get Hank to help me retrieve the carcass and bring it over to the vet."

JoJo looked at Crew. He stood, his hands in the pockets of his grimy jacket, dark hair curling out of the back of a gimme cap, unshaven, looking at her through thick eyelashes, and she had the sense that there was more, much more, to this man than just a guy who'd saved her life. So, "Can I buy you a pizza?"

"Depends on the kind of pizza."

She cocked an eyebrow. "Pepperoni?"

"Add some onions and green peppers and I'm all yours."

"Wow, you're easy."

"I'm hungry." But he winked again and headed for the door.

And suddenly, she was too. Maybe not for pizza.

They walked across the street to Starlight Pizza, all lit up with outdoor lights around a patio deck with picnic tables and music from a guy seated on a stool, strumming a guitar. They sat at a yellow-painted table, and she looked at the standup menu. "Today's special is Hawaiian."

"I'd rather be dragged behind stampeding caribou."

She looked up at him.

He shrugged. "Just sayin' that pizza shouldn't come with fruit."

"I couldn't agree more."

He grinned then and shed his jacket. Underneath, he wore a brown thermal shirt, formfitting over his shoulders, his chest.

She put him about her age, maybe, youth in his face despite whatever years he wore in his eyes.

"So how do you know so much about wolves? Are you a biologist or something?" he asked.

"Hoping to be. Working on my master's thesis on the mating and long-term monogamy of wolves."

A waitress came over. Blonde, maybe early college age. "Hey. I'm Parker. Have you decided?"

"Large deep-dish pepperoni, onions, green peppers. A pitcher of lemonade. And it's on me," Crew said.

JoJo stared at him. "That wasn't—" She looked at Parker. "It's on me."

"I'll let you two wrestle that out." She walked away, and JoJo gave Crew a look.

"What?" Crew shrugged. "You got hit on the head. You're not thinking clearly."

"I got on the back of an ATV with you, didn't I?"

"My point exactly." But he grinned.

Shoot, he was cute. "So, how is it that you appeared from nowhere to save my life?"

Parker came back with the pitcher, two cups, straws. He popped his paper off with a hit on the table. "I have land nearby. I was, um . . . looking for trouble."

"Like wolves?" She stirred her lemonade.

"Or pretty, slightly bossy women."

She sat back. "Oh no. You are a stalker."

He held up a hand. "Never said I found one."

She smiled.

He did too. It lit up his entire face, added depth to his eyes, a sort of infectious humor to his countenance, and right then, she stopped hurting, just a little.

At the very least, he was playing with fire.

Any one of the Sons of Revolution showed up in town, and he'd be made. And with him, JoJo. Because Crew knew—absolutely knew in his gut—that the mysterious "poison" that had killed Brutus had to be the necrotoxin.

He'd eaten the dead salmon, and it had somehow affected his nervous system.

The thought nearly threw off Crew's appetite, but he'd do anything for pizza, so he finished a couple pieces, eyed a third.

Nope.

Because if he finished it off, the night might end. And he liked her laugh. Her eyes. And maybe he simply hadn't seen a beautiful woman for a while—count, a year—but JoJo could stop his heart with her smile.

And there was the little problem of not leaving town until he talked with Rio. Crew had sent him a text when he'd arrived in town, but so far, no answer. At least, not when he surreptitiously glanced at his phone now and again.

C'mon, Rio. "So, you followed Dr. Samson all the way to Alaska from Montana?"

"She's been doing revolutionary work with the wolves. Did you know that usually, in a pack, only the alpha male and alpha female mate? The rest of the pack are there for protection and food. But they all work together."

Across the deck, the singer had started a new song—a country ballad. Something romantic. Sheesh, his brain was stuck.

"They also have incredible stamina. They can travel twenty miles for food. And their howl—it helps bring back lost wolves and even establish territory."

"And scares anyone sleeping out in the bush."

She took a sip. "That too. I remember the first time I heard a wolf howl. I was out with my dad—maybe about seven or eight years old. We were camping in Yellowstone, and a wolf howled. So mournful. Made the hairs on my neck stand on end."

"Yellowstone. Never been there."

"I grew up in the area. My parents were wild-life biologists studying the wolf population. The wolves were a real problem in Montana, especially with the ranchers, so they landed on the endangered species list for a while. My parents tracked them enough to watch them repopulate. They were taken off the list in 2014." She looked away then, something playing on her face. She sighed.

He frowned. "What was that?"

She looked back, her mouth open. "Oh. Sorry. I was thinking about . . . well, a dog I had."

"A dog—wait, a wolf dog?"

"Actually, yes. Two generations south of a pure-bred. Her name was Dakota. She was killed in 2014, mistaken for a wolf."

"I'm sorry."

She nodded, sighed. "Wouldn't have been so bad, but she was killed by a neighbor who knew her and just didn't trust her."

His mouth closed. He nodded. He knew a little about neighborhood betrayal.

A man entered the deck area. He sat at a table, his cap low. Crew glanced at him.

"Anyway, never had the urge to get another

dog, but I did decide to study them. After I graduate, I want to move here full time. Work for the park service."

Yes, definitely Rio, with his dark hair, solid build. He looked at Crew, nodded.

"So, do you own a ranch or something?" JoJo asked.

He looked at her, tried to wrap her words into his head. "Ranch?"

"Or are you a . . . like, a homesteader?"

Oh, right. "Yes. Sort of. I work security for a small . . . uh, farm, out in the bush." Shoot, usually he was better at this lying game.

"Security. Oh, that makes sense."

He looked at her.

"The .308. And you managed to miss me, so that's a win."

He smiled. "Definitely."

Was that a blush? Forget Rio, the woman had his full attention. "So, do you work for the park service now?"

She shook her head. "No, I'm with—"

"JoJo! What are you doing here?"

The voice made him turn, and he froze.

Cover. Blown. Shoot. Except—

"Skye. Hey." Across from him, JoJo got up, gave Skye Parker, Rio's wife, a hug.

Sweat chilled his spine.

"What are you doing here?" Skye said and then turned to Crew, who'd also stood up. She raised an eyebrow.

"Long story. This is Crew. I met him ... well ... in the woods. And it's not how it sounds."

"Crew," Skye said. "Nice to meet you."

"You too, ma'am." He nodded his head.

Skye narrowed her eyes at him, glanced at JoJo. And he could practically read her mind.

Stay. Away.

Don't get her mixed up in this.

And then his entire body turned cold. Wait—

"I'm headed back up to base camp after we're done with our pizza," JoJo said.

Oh no, she was a firefighter.

"Base camp?" he asked, his gut clenching.

"With the Midnight Sun fire crew. I'm a smokejumper."

He put a hand on the table, just in case his knees decided to betray him. He kept his smile, glanced at Rio.

Talk. *Now.*

Because, ahem, the same smokejumpers that the Sons of Revolution wanted to track down and kill? He hadn't been a part of the chase that'd downed the Midnight Sun jump plane, but he'd heard about it, back at their new camp.

He'd been busy moving their gear and setting up at a new camp after said smokejumpers, um, blew up their old camp.

So yeah, the entire crew wore a target on their yellow Nomex-shirted backs.

Rio had gotten up even as Crew climbed out of his seat. "Feel free to sit down. I'll be right back," he said to Skye, then looked at JoJo.

Maybe a little too long. Because he didn't want to say goodbye. Didn't want the light that she seemed to ignite inside him to wink out.

"Are you leaving?" she asked.

Was that the tiniest sliver of hope in her voice?

It opened up a terrible hole inside, and suddenly he was sucking air. He shook his head. "I'll be back."

"Good. Because I'm driving you back to your ATV there, champ."

Oh.

He nearly put a hand to his chest as he walked away, the tug to stay so strong.

Walking out onto the sidewalk, he passed the pizza joint, then turned and headed down a side street, then over into the woods behind Starlight.

Rio waited in the shadows in a stand of trees.

Crew joined him, turned, and spotted JoJo talking with Skye on the patio, under the blinking lights.

Rio grabbed him, pulled him away from the sight. "What are you doing?"

He rounded on him, cuffed away his hold on his arm. "What am I doing? What are you doing bringing your wife here? Sheesh—she knows me, man."

"And I can trust her to keep her mouth shut about our little party. But you—any one of the SOR could see you here."

"Who cares—"

"With a smokejumper."

Rio wore a beard, and with his dark eyes and dark hair, the canvas jacket, he resembled every inch of the man Crew had met at the Copper Mountain Correctional Facility. Of course, Rio had been undercover at the time.

Crew, not so much.

Now Rio could be just as deceptive, just as tough, just as scary as he'd been as an FBI agent trying to protect and eke out information from an informant, way back in the day.

Except he also considered Crew to be a sort of little brother, so now he unhanded him. "You okay?"

"Yeah."

"Last I heard was a gunshot."

"Wolf attack. Not me. But I think I figured out the SOR's bigger plan."

Rio folded his arms.

"Food supply. They dosed the salmon, and JoJo thinks that the wolf ate the salmon, got sick."

Rio was nodding. "They also sprayed a homestead near the Refuge. Killed the chickens, and the woman had some sort of toxic reaction." He ran a hand behind his head. "Are you any closer to figuring out where they're storing this, or even how they're making it?"

"No. I know there's more than one location. Jer is back—he disappeared not long after I embedded. He came back a few weeks ago. And Viper has taken over after Howards's death."

"Tristan."

"Yeah. He killed him trying to get his sister and her friend Logan out. How is he?"

"Dunno. He went off the radar after he was found in a fire. Went to the hospital, then AWOL. Probably laying low."

"Or dead."

Rio's mouth made a tight line. He nodded. Then glanced past him to JoJo. "She was on the property?"

"Nearly."

He sighed. "The SOR still hunting the SJs?"

"There's talk." Crew turned, spotted her in the light. So pretty, and laughing, and something simply grabbed him, squeezed.

Desire, maybe. "I'm tired of this, boss. I've been embedded for over a year and . . ."

A hand clamped on his shoulder, and he glanced back at Rio.

The man nodded, his eyes kind. "I know. I get it. More than you can imagine. We just need to find out the bigger picture and stop them. And if you can locate the warehouse, that would go a long way to shutting down this bioweapon."

"They have me on patrol, but that's all."

"Which means you need to get back before they start wondering where you are."

He sighed, nodded.

"I'll drive you." Rio urged him toward the dirt street, away from Starlight.

"I need to say goodbye—"

"No, you don't. It'll only make it harder. Trust me on this."

Crew turned, his gaze on JoJo. *I'll be back.*

Sorry, Jo.

He stood for a long moment, then turned and

followed Rio through the shadows and away from the light.

THREE

S HE HADN'T EXACTLY PRAYED FOR fire—no one did that. But to be honest, the noise of their new Twin Otter aircraft, the quiet tension as the Midnight Sun jumpers sat in the belly, simply drilled out the question that wouldn't stop thrumming inside.

Why had he left?

No word, just walked away into the sunny night and never returned.

She'd waited with Skye, finished her pizza, listened to music, waited some more. Skye's husband Rio had even shown up after about forty-five minutes, looking for her.

JoJo couldn't look at Skye as they left and she realized she'd been stood up.

Fine. Whatever.

She moved her hands over her equipment. The ram-air chute main toggle, the reserve toggle, her harness, snapped and secured, the altimeter strapped to her wrist—nearly at thirty-five-hundred feet. Radio and GPS secure in her leg pocket, fire shelter in the other leg pocket, and in her pouch pack, a first aid kit, flashlight, and overnight gear—just in case the fire was bigger than the reports.

Just a small fire started by lightning—still under an acre, but it threatened power lines and a cluster of cabins near the Denali High Adventure Scout Base. Just a quick putdown. They'd cut a line and conduct a burnout ahead of the fire, cut another contingency line to the south, but the rest of the fire raged in a limited management area.

Nature would take care of it as it headed north into the park.

As Jade had explained their action plan, JoJo had studied the map and realized the fire wasn't terribly far from Brutus and Cleo's old den.

And now, shoot—there he was, Crew, hopping into her brain, driving up on a four-wheeler, the lumberjack version of Batman.

Stop.

Their pilot, Neil, motioned to their spotter, a man named Mark, and Jade moved forward. The two opened the door and pointed out their drop area.

They dropped the ribbon, and JoJo watched it spiral out, saw the wind grab it, churn it away from the puff of smoke spiraling up from the dense clutter of trees. No flames peeking through the gray, so maybe the fire hadn't started to crown yet.

The crew helped them with the gear box as Neil circled, and Mark and Jade sent that out to the drop zone.

Then Jade turned to her crew.

"Nobody dies today!" Her talisman shout-out.

They responded with a thumbs-up, and then Logan got up and started their prejump chant. "The Lord himself goes before you and will be with you!"

JoJo took her place beside Logan, and the others lined up behind them as they finished the chant. She glanced at Logan as he shouted, "Do not be discouraged!" Then he nodded to her, his jaw tight.

Jade unclipped their safety lines, and in a second, JoJo started the count.

Jump thousand.

The air caught her, and every single time, it felt like leaping off into freedom. A crazy, ethereal exhilaration caught her breath, and despite the wind in her ears, cutting out sound, she reveled in it.

Look thousand.

The world, at this moment, belonged to her. Hers to control, to live or die. From here, the world seemed less cluttered, more expansive, and she spotted caribou running along distant tundra, the rising furry peaks of the foothills, and the dark granite of the massive Alaska Range jutting, sharp and rugged, from the earth.

And for a second, Crew and his cold exit dropped away from her brain.

To the northeast, the forest balded, turning into rock as if God had already precut the line. To the southwest, Whisper Creek. The fire to the east, the camp to the west—if they cut a line between the bald spot and the creek, burned it out, they could drive it back to the Copper River.

Reach thousand.

She glanced at Logan, who also flew, twenty feet away. Reached for her primary toggle. Found it, buffeted by the wind. Grabbed it. Her gaze fell on the river to the west. Too far to see the cliff. But the sun glinted off something in the distance, maybe a half click from the river, north, where a splinter river flowed into the Copper.

Maybe five miles from the village they'd helped evacuate about a week ago.

Wait thousand.

She focused on the fire, spotted it now, flaring up between trees, growing, the smoke churning into the sky. Smelled it—acrid and crisp, the air turning heated. Now the adrenaline pooled in her gut, the dragon roaring, a low hum of warning.

Pull thousand.

The jerk shot her up as the chute deployed, and she caught her toggles, sitting in her harness, driving.

She loved this part.

Logan, too, had deployed his chute and now pointed at their landing spot. He seemed less driven lately, and maybe his new girlfriend, Jamie, had something to do with that.

I'll be right back.

Nope.

The earth loomed closer, and she angled her chute, catching the wind, riding it northeast toward the drop zone. *I've had harder falls, believe me.*

Oh, for Pete's sake.

Logan came in, and she watched as he landed, rolled, popped back up.

Perfect.

She yanked hard on her toggles, slowed her descent, and landed, almost like a whisper, running and then rolling, textbook.

She came up, grabbed her chute, and ran toward the gear box Mark had deployed. As the rest of the team landed, they broke out the Pulaskis and chain saws and drip torches.

Jade landed and ran over, unlatching her harness as she ran. "Let's get moving. We need to build that line, start the backfire."

The hum and crackle of fire ate into her words. Not a roar yet.

But soon, if they didn't hurry.

She grabbed her Pulaski, headed out after Logan, and stopped thinking.

Eight hours later, fatigue ate at her brain, her entire body wrung out, hurting, her lungs raw, her hands hot under her gloves—probably a few blisters forming—and her feet raw. Dirt and soot streaked her face, and she sat on the bald spot above the fire, surveying the land, drinking from her warm water bottle.

Smoke spiraled from where the two fires fought for life—not happening, not after the line they'd dug, the backfire they'd deployed. It ate at the main blaze and shut down the advance. Jade had called in a chopper of shots to mop up and to pick up the team.

She preferred sleeping in her cot back at the base instead of the hard, charred ground, thank you.

Taking off her helmet, she poured water over her head, let it soak into her hair, run down her face.

"Sheesh, Jo, that's a look." Skye came over, plopped down beside her.

"I'm not trying to impress anyone." She wiped her face with her scarf, probably rubbing ash into her pores.

"I'm impressed." This from Hammer, who glanced over at her, winked.

She rolled her eyes.

"Not even . . . Crew ?" Skye angled a look at her.

Aw. She'd gone eight entire hours without thinking about him. She shook her head. "He ghosted me. We're done. And . . . we never started. He—"

"Saved your life. That sounds like a good start."

She lifted a shoulder. "Whatever. I don't know what it was. But . . . no, I'm not interested."

"Even if he had a good reason?" Skye capped her water bottle.

She looked over at Skye. "Why, you know something?"

Skye frowned, shook her head. "Why would I know anything?"

JoJo frowned, but she was right. Why would she? She sighed. "No. Any guy who ghosts me after he promises to come back can't be trusted. I don't date people I don't trust." She lifted a shoulder. "And I'm too busy anyway."

"Right." Skye hung her hands over her knees. "Any word on that wolf and how he died?"

"Dunno." In fact, she'd gotten a buzz on her phone right before they'd deployed. She reached into her leg pocket now and pulled it out. Thumbed open her text.

Peyton.

Peyton
Picked up Cleo's track. Her patterns suggest a den nearby. I dropped a pin.

JoJo clicked on it. The pin spun and spun, loading.

"No signal." She showed Skye.

"They have cell service at base camp on Denali. Stand up."

"I look ridiculous." But she stood, held the phone in the air.

And then, just like that, it loaded.

"Huh." She sat and showed Skye. Stilled. "That's not far from here. South, like a few miles past Whisper Creek." She zoomed out. "There're no roads into there."

"You'd have to take a four-wheeler."

"I could have the chopper drop me off, then hike to the river." She pointed to a dirt road along the river.

"And who is going to pick you up at the river road? Some lumberjack?"

Lumberjack Batman?

Aw.

"I'll pick you up," Hammer said, grinning, white teeth against his sooted face.

"Really?"

"Just give me a call when you're ready."

Overhead, a chopper beat the sky, distant, carrying in reinforcements.

She climbed to her feet. Looked at Skye. "Why not? I'm already packed."

He should have eaten that last piece of pizza. And wasn't that a strange regret lifting out of the stew of so many regrets? The most recent being his promise-breaking. But he just couldn't stop thinking about . . .

Well, what if.

He didn't know where to start with the what-ifs, really.

Maybe it started with the moment he'd ended up in camp, late and in trouble, with Viper asking him where he'd been.

He'd told him the truth—wolf attack, disposal of the body, and did he know that maybe the wolf had eaten poisoned salmon?

Not a hint of remorse from Viper. But it'd worked, and he'd managed not to go a couple rounds with the alpha jerk and climb into his bunk in the communal sleeping room.

His brain stuck on JoJo, of course.

JoJo and her beautiful hazel-green eyes, that long brown hair, her laughter.

Sheesh, his chest hurt, even now.

Focus on the lock, work the pins, just like he'd learned.

Maybe it'd started with what if he hadn't de-cided to skip dinner and offer to take an extra surveillance shift, giving him a small—very small—window to break into Viper's office and root around.

If you can locate the warehouse, that would go a long way to shutting down this bioweapon.

Yeah, and the sooner he could breathe again.

Footsteps in the main area, and he stilled, but they walked by, probably on the way to the latrines out back.

He crouched, kept fidgeting with the lock.

From the main room, conversation lifted, loud, raucous, crude. And maybe he didn't really miss dinner. He couldn't stomach another round of moose stew.

The door creaked open, and he scurried into the room, shut the door, and pulled a flashlight from his pocket.

The map on Peyton's wall had jogged a memory. Back in their first camp, a map had hung on the wall of Howards's office.

He shone a light on the table shoved against the wall, the one Viper used as a desk.

I'm tired of this, boss. I've been embedded for over a year.

Maybe he'd go further back to Rio's great idea to insert him into the SOR like he might be one of these thugs. He'd been so—too—idealistic back then.

Focus.

The light fell on a couple schematics. Looked

like a plane, maybe. And another—a grid with a colored pattern, starting dark in the middle, lighter at the edges.

Footsteps outside, and he cut the light. No windows in this room, but that also meant no escape.

If Viper found him in here, snooping around, he'd beat him until he talked—which he wouldn't—and then he'd kill him. Slowly.

Maybe let Jer do it.

Oh, he hated this place.

No, if he were peeling back the what-ifs, it would be the moment his stupid cousin, Aaron, had suggested a joyride in Ben Barrett's 1994 T-roof Corvette.

He closed his eyes, listening to the footsteps stop. Outside the door. Voices.

"He'll be here in four days. Just sit tight until then. No moves until the big guy gets here."

The doorknob rattled, and Crew searched for a weapon. Maybe the straight chair and, yes, Rio's crash course in personal defense, not to mention Crew's short stint in lockup, had taught him a few things, but—

No. He was going to die.

And it was going to hurt.

And he'd never get a chance to say goodbye.

To tell JoJo that ... yeah, okay, ever so briefly, life hadn't felt so dark.

Maybe not dark at all.

A curse. "Forgot my key."

He blew out a breath as the footsteps left. Then he crept to the door, opened it, and rolled into the dark hallway.

No one standing sentry, and he nearly stopped breathing. Instead, he found his feet, headed to the security office, and slipped inside.

Turned back on the camera to the office—no harm, no foul—and maybe no one would notice the missing minutes.

He sat, sweat prickling his spine, his hands on the chair, staring at the screens. Heard Rio's voice. *We just need to find out the bigger picture and stop them.*

Four days.

"Crew?"

He nearly shot out of his seat, jumped anyway. Turned.

Viper stood in the now open doorway. Dark hair, shaved short, with a scar across his cheek, pale blue eyes, built like a moose, skinny legs, power in his torso. He could hit like a bulldozer—Crew had felt it, early days, training.

The man had emptied Crew's stomach on more than one occasion.

"Hey. Just wanted to say good job on the wolf kill. We traced it to a couple of idiots who poured some chemical waste into the river upstream. Killed a bunch of salmon. We dealt with them."

Crew raised an eyebrow.

"Gotta protect the land, right?" He held out a fist. Crew bumped it.

Whatever.

"Boss. We got a perimeter breach."

Viper opened the door. Jer stood there, a wreck of a man despite his relative youth, the drug use and large living hard on his body, a snake tattoo curling up around his neck. Clearly he had some high-up connections that made Viper keep him around.

"You see anything, Crew?"

Shoot. "Nothing on-screen, sir." He hoped. But he turned, got up. "Where was it?"

"Over by the river. Rocco is bringing her in."

Her.

No, it couldn't be her. Maybe it was a tourist, a hiker who'd wandered into the wrong area. A fly fisher—um, woman.

"It's one of them smokejumpers."

Ice fell through him. Crew got up.

Viper held out his hand. "You sit tight, Crew. I'll meet him." He turned to Jer. "With me."

Crew stood, frozen, as Viper walked out, shut the door.

He dropped into the chair, his hands white on the arms, and turned to the screen.

No, God, please—his gaze stayed on the front gate, his stomach churning.

He spotted the four-wheelers coming back in—two of them out on perimeter patrol, probably one meeting up with the other. And on the grainy black-and-white screen, a person, tied up, hands behind her back.

She wore boots and a jacket and a backpack and a bandana and . . .

And as they hauled her up, her long braid swung out.

He was on his feet, the chair slamming back.

She stood, feet out, as if angry—he knew that look—jerking away from Rocco's hold. Lifted her chin as Viper came into the screen.

If he hit her, even once, he'd break her skull.

Crew slammed open the door, took off down the hallway, through the main hall, out the front door.

The sun hung low—he guessed the hour nearly midnight—and glinted off the metal Quonset hut that housed their vehicles—the four-wheelers, the snowmobiles, a couple trucks. A few smaller, private cabins were for Viper, and others for visitors. They'd had a couple since Crew's arrival.

A training area, mandatory, held pull-up bars, a high wall, and a boxing ring.

And facing the vehicle building, in another Quonset hut, an armory. Because, you know, peaceful lumberjacks in the woods needed a stash of AR-15s, AK-47s, and Ruger 10/22 semiautomatics. A Barrett .50 sniper rifle, and he'd even spotted a M249 SAW, probably for when the FBI sieged them. They also had tactical lights and laser sights and night vision scopes—if the SEALs ever ran out of gear.

A chain-link perimeter circled the entire compound, razor wire at the top.

Yeah, it gave him fresh nightmares every time he stepped outside.

But he ignored it all now, crossing the compound at a full run.

Viper stood in front of JoJo, and Crew winced as duct tape was ripped from her mouth. Oh, that had to hurt. Hopefully she was smart and had loosened it with saliva before it'd been torn from her skin.

And that thought had him skidding, stopping, breathing hard, slowing to a walk.

Because the last thing he wanted was to land on the wrong side here. *Think, Crew.*

"Who are you, and what are you doing on my property?" Viper, low, menacing.

"You're the one who poisoned the wolf, aren't you?"

Oh, Jo, stop talking.

"Oh, I see. You came snooping around hoping to find—"

"Me."

And it just fell out of his mouth, easy, like the answer had always belonged there. But as soon as he said it, the entire plan formed, just like that.

As if it might be meant to be.

"She came looking for me."

And right then, JoJo turned, her mouth opening slightly, her eyes widening. She gasped. "Crew?"

Yeah, baby, way to play along.

He walked right up to her, took her face in his hands, met her eyes, and nodded. "Hey, honey. Sorry I vanished on you. I missed you."

And then he kissed her.

Kissed her like he meant it, as if he'd longed to

see her, as if they belonged to each other, as if her showing up had saved his life.

And maybe, just maybe, it had.

She smelled of fire and ash, tasted of coffee, and in his arms, she relaxed.

And, ever so briefly, kissed him back.

That was enough.

He let her go, turned, looked at Viper. "Sorry. I should have told you. This is Jo—my girlfriend."

Viper stared at him, so much in his eyes that Crew didn't want to take it apart. "Your girlfriend is a smokejumper."

Crew raised an eyebrow, glanced at her and back to Viper. He motioned with his head and cut his voice low.

Viper followed him.

"C'mon, Viper. What, did you think I'd let these guys get away?"

Viper frowned.

He glanced at Jo, back to Viper.

"You're playing her?"

"Trust me. You want the smokejumpers, she'll lead us to them." Then he winked.

And Viper smiled.

And for the first time in days, Crew stopped what-iffing and started to hope.

Because the light was back.

FOUR

WHAT JUST HAPPENED?" AT LEAST she was keeping her voice down as Crew walked her to the guest cabin. He glanced back at Viper, still watching them, and opened the door.

JoJo glanced up at him, her jaw tight.

"Trust me, please," he whispered, and she narrowed her eyes but stepped inside.

He closed the door behind her.

The late evening cast shadows into the room through a half-boarded window. A simple one-person cot—it looked out of a World War II movie, with a canvas top and wooden frame—was pushed up against one wall, a simple wooden table and two straight chairs against another.

"Are we in some Russian gulag? What is this place?"

She seemed to be shaking a little, and he didn't blame her. Crew took her by the arms, met her eyes. "I'll explain everything." Then he turned her, pulled out a knife, and cut her zip ties.

She rubbed her wrists, met his eyes.

And for a second, the kiss rose up in her beautiful hazel-green eyes. Maybe it had been a little more real than he'd intended. He'd tried to be gentle, to keep the desperation out of it, to ask her, with it, to go along with him. To remember her words to him—*I'm going to choose to trust you, Crew.*

Please.

He stepped back from her. "First, I'm sorry I ghosted you in Copper Mountain."

Her mouth opened, closed. "That is the last thing I care about right now."

Right.

"You okay?" He met her eyes, and it seemed like she'd been crying. Why not? A couple thugs had grabbed her, tied her up, and given her a harrowing ride on the back of an ATV. But her expression remained fierce, sturdy.

"Did they hurt you?" His gaze fixed on hers.

She drew in a breath. "Not much."

Not much.

He closed his eyes then, and the cold knot inside him uncoiled, just a little. *Thank You, Lord.* He opened his eyes. "Thank you for trusting me in the yard."

"For not calling you out when you called me your girlfriend?"

He lifted a shoulder. "Sorry. I didn't know what to do."

"Yeah, well, Thug in Charge looked like he wanted to strangle me—and you, so . . . I don't know. I went with it."

She looked away, though, as if shaken.

He went over to her, again touched her shoulders. "It's going to be okay. Please trust me."

She looked back at him, shook her head, stepped out of his grip. "You ghost me in Copper Mountain, and now you kiss me in the middle of a war camp. I think aside from running away screaming, trust is my only choice."

Right.

"What's going on, Crew?"

He stepped back from her and leaned on the small table. "Welcome to the Sons of Revolution."

"The what?"

"It's a group of militia who want to bring

America back to the early days—no electricity, live off the land, Wild West law."

"And you're with them?" Her voice rose a little, and he held up a hand. She went back to a whisper. "Seriously?"

He cut his own voice low, almost inaudible. "No. I've been embedded with them for over a year, trying to figure out what their larger plan is."

"Embedded? Wait—you're—"

"One of the good guys." His mouth made a grim, tight line. "Or trying to be."

She wrapped her arms around herself and looked around the cabin. "What is this, the dungeon?"

"It used to be an old camp. I think it was a Christian camp—there are quite a few verses cut into the logs, and the old chapel is our barracks. This used to be a campers' cabin. Now it's the guest quarters. I talked Viper into letting you stay here."

"I'm not staying here." She rounded back to him. "My team is going to get worried."

He had perched on the table, leaning against it, his hands folded. "I'll figure out a way to get you out. It's just going to take some creativity. But I promise, I won't let anything happen to you." He kept his tone soft, maybe a little earnest, and perhaps it found her, because she sighed, released her tight hold on herself.

Then, "Creativity?"

"They're rather paranoid about anyone knowing where their camp is." He raised an eyebrow. "If you'll remember, the last one went up in flames."

Her mouth opened. "Right." She looked at her attire. "I came straight from a fire."

"Clearly." He ran a hand across his mouth. "You probably want a shower."

She looked at herself. Met his eyes. "Only if it doesn't involve getting ogled by a camp of men."

"I think I can guarantee privacy." Or he hoped so. "I didn't see a fire. Where is the rest of your team?"

"It was north of here about ten miles. Small. We got it, and they choppered out about four hours ago. I got a ping from Peyton about Cleo and the pups and asked to be dropped off. I've been looking for them ever since."

Of course she had. "Just tromping around the woods in the middle of the night."

"It's not the middle of the night, and Hammer said he'd pick me up. I wasn't that far from the road."

"Hammer?" And he didn't like the way the name sat inside him, a boulder.

Hello, she *wasn't* his girlfriend, and he should probably remember that.

"A guy on the team. I was supposed to walk out to the road and radio him when I needed pickup."

"Tonight?"

She shook her head. "I told him I'd probably sleep in the rough. I had a backpack before your guys took it from me."

"Not my guys," he growled. "I'm not one of them, JoJo."

Her mouth tightened, and she looked away. Wiped her cheek.

Aw. He stepped back up to her, touched her arm. "I'm not going to let anything happen to you."

She looked back at him, and he couldn't stop himself. He put his arms around her, pulled her sooty body to himself.

And for a moment—a delicious, perfect moment—she let him hold her. Even relaxed against him, put an arm around his waist. "I guess, thank you again for saving my life, Batman."

He hadn't a clue what she meant by that, but, "Here to protect and serve."

She gave a tiny laugh, and it rumbled through her body into his, and again, just like that, the darkness broke open, lifted.

As if God had heard his prayers.

She pushed away then and pulled the handkerchief off her hair. "I'd take you up on your shower idea, but I don't have a change of clothes."

"I can take care of that." He didn't hate the idea of her in his clothes.

Stop. Not a girlfriend.

"Did you find the pups?"

She sank onto the cot. He'd have to get her a sleeping bag too.

"No. But I did find something, and probably that's why I got picked up." She reached into her leg pocket and pulled out a mangled weed sprig with a few black berries. Set it on the cot next to her. "A greenhouse. Full of these."

"Weeds?"

"*Atropa belladonna.*"

"What?"

"Nightshade berries. Death berries, we call them in the biology field. They're poisonous, extremely toxic when ingested. They can cause hallucinations and delirium and, taken in the right quantities, death."

He picked up the sprig. "You found a greenhouse with these?"

"Yeah. When we were jumping into the fire, I spotted a metal building, and when the chopper dropped me off, I saw it again. It wasn't far from the den, so I thought—I don't know. I thought maybe it was a homestead, you know? Anyway, I got inside, and there are hundreds, maybe a thousand plants. All in berry. I took a sample. I don't know why."

He stared at it. "Could this be what your wolf ate?"

"Brutus. I don't know. Animals eat these all the time, and it doesn't kill them."

But if it was used in some other chemical concoction . . .

"Can you show me where you got this?"

"Sure." She stood up.

"Not tonight." He glanced toward the door. "For sure they'll be watching you. Us. I'll figure out how to get away. For now, let's get you cleaned up."

"It's not a group activity."

"It is here." He stood up. "Wait here. I'll be back."

Her eyes widened, and she drew in a breath. And shoot—his words at the pizza place washed over him. He turned, stepped up to her. "Listen. I know you're freaking out, and the last thing you want to be is my girlfriend. But if Viper and the rest of the guys know you're with me, then . . . well, hopefully they'll leave you alone."

"Hopefully?"

"They mess with you, they mess with me."

Her eyebrow rose. "Now you really sound like Batman. What are you going to do? Fight the compound for my honor?" She smiled.

Oh, and the desire to kiss her just swelled over him, nearly took possession. His gaze even flickered to her mouth, then back to her eyes.

He blew out a breath, nodded, stepped back. "If I have to." Then he winked and headed for the door. "Lock this behind me. And don't let anyone but me back in."

Then he stepped out into the night and prayed his words didn't come true.

She just might live through the night.

Freezing, and nearly hypothermic, but alive. And the wool blanket Crew had given her helped.

Still, her soot-free wet hair was plastered against her skin, and she shivered, despite the blanket and being dressed for the dead of winter in an oversized pair of canvas pants, a thermal shirt that came down to her knees, and a thick flannel shirt.

Crew's clothing, no doubt, because it sort of smelled like him—a woodsy, rugged scent, enriched with the homemade soap she'd used on her hair and body in the rough-hewn communal shower in a building with a cement floor and dim lighting. Crew had stood sentry at the door, but she'd taken the fastest shower in history under water that had frozen her to the bone.

So, that was ultra fun.

In truth, the entire last six hours had her head spinning, from the chase-down by the thugs on their ATVs, to the harrowing ride on the back of the ATV, to her knee-buckling face-off with Viper, to . . . Crew.

She could barely get her brain around his appearance, his explanation—embedded?—his lie, and then . . . the kiss.

Yeah, that stuck in her brain, a sort of marker where life had stilled. And in that moment, she'd gathered herself, the screaming inside silencing, her shaking stilling.

She blamed his gentleness and the fact that, regardless of why he'd kissed her, it hadn't felt fake. And in that moment, all she'd been able to think was . . . *I'm going to choose to trust you, Crew.*

So she'd kissed him back.

And didn't regret it. Not one little bit as he

sat, now on the floor, tucked into a sleeping bag, across from where she perched on the cot.

He'd dragged in the bag and thrown it on the wood-planked floor when he'd escorted her back to the cabin. The boards had creaked when he'd sat on the bag, a couple of them rattling. Sunlight fell through the wooden boards of the window.

"No way am I letting you sleep in here alone," he'd said, leaning against the wall, folding his arms. Didn't look like he was going to sleep either.

And while her mother might not love her sharing a cabin with her, um, *boyfriend*, she wasn't about to kick him out. Not with the cadre of rough-edged men outside, who had watched her as she'd trekked back to the cabin, soggy, shivering, and maybe a little fragile.

I'm one of the good guys.

Yes, this much about him, she knew, was true. The rest . . .

"How did you end up here?" she asked.

He sat with his eyes closed, his head back against the wall as if wrung out, and it hit her that if he wasn't one of these thugs—probably not—then he'd been forced to act like them to fit in.

And even pretending to be darkness could seep

into a person's soul. No wonder he looked tired. And handsome.

Terribly, perfectly handsome, with that dark beard and a toned frame that had made her believe him when he'd said that anyone who wanted to hurt her had to go through him.

Yeah, Mr. Michael Crew Sterling had secrets. And she wanted to unlock them.

Now, he opened his eyes to her question. Sighed. "It's a long story."

"Sun's still up."

He laughed, a deep, low rumble that ended in a wry smile. "It's midnight."

"So, tell me a bedtime story."

He swallowed, and even in the dim light, he seemed almost . . . embarrassed?

"It can't be that bad."

"I was in jail."

Oh.

He met her gaze. "I stole a car."

"Why?"

He frowned, gave a huff. "Uh, they never really asked me that, but the answer is, my cousin Aaron said it would be fun. It was my neighbor's Corvette. He never drove it—it just sat in his driveway, a vintage car getting moldy. He was out of town, and Aaron said, 'Let's take it out.' And I was a stupid eighteen-year-old kid with no brains, and I said yes. So we broke in, hotwired it, and took it joyriding."

"Doesn't sound like a jail-worthy offense."

"I crashed it."

Her mouth made an O.

"Yeah. It was actually drivable, and I returned it to Ben and promised to pay for it. And I thought we were good, but a prosecutor caught me on camera and decided to make an example out of me. Ben wrote a letter to the court, and they only sentenced me to three months, but it was a felony, so yeah. Not a great start to life."

She didn't want to think about him, eighteen years old, in prison. "Is that where you learned to fight?"

He raised an eyebrow.

"'They'll have to go through me.'" She finger quoted the words.

He gave a short huff. "Yeah. No. My dad taught me."

"Your dad?"

"Yeah. He was a Marine. Cool. Broken. Came back from Iraq all screwed up. Did some local boxing for cash. Ended up in a bar fight, killed a man, went to jail for manslaughter."

She stared at him. "Oh, I'm so sorry."

"Yeah. Funny thing was, when I went to jail, he was there. So we had some father-son bonding time." He shook his head. "That's where he taught me to fight and pretty much looked out for me. Introduced me to Rio."

Her mouth opened. "Skye's husband."

He dropped his voice, glanced at the door. "He's my handler."

Right. She nodded, also dropped her voice. "No wonder Skye sat with me such a long time at Starlight Pizza. Did you have a meet?"

"Sort of. We're trying to figure out what the endgame of SOR is. We know they're developing a biochemical weapon. We just don't know the plan."

"The nightshade greenhouse—do you think they're using it to make a bioweapon?"

"I'd like to take a look at it. I have a plan to sneak out tomorrow."

His words sank into her. "How dangerous are these guys? If they find us missing—"

"Very dangerous." He made a grim face. "You saw how they came after your team, right?"

She nodded. "They remind me of the guys who killed my father." Oh—what? She hadn't quite meant for that to emerge, but—

"Killed your father?"

"Poachers. He tried to stop them from killing a pack of wolves." She shook her head. "I was nine years old. He was my whole world." Wow, that was probably way too much information. But sitting here in the semidarkness, wrapped in a blanket, Crew quiet and listening, his earlier words lingering in her mind—*I'm one of the good guys*—it felt easy.

"I'm so sorry."

"It was just me and my mom after that. I was their only child—they had me late in life. Mom is still a field research biologist. She works for Yellowstone, overseeing the bear and bison population—health and protection, and even interaction with tourists."

Crew's dark eyes had pinned to her, a hint of what looked like sweet concern on his face. Or maybe she just hoped it.

Sheesh. Not his girlfriend. Hello.

"Sounds like a strong woman."

"Absolutely. I remember standing at his graveside, the rain pouring down. It was autumn, a hint of chill in the air, the trees letting go of their leaves, a sort of loamy smell mixed with dirt, and I just couldn't get my eyes off the coffin, the hole. And my mom squeezed my hand and said, 'This darkness will not consume us, Joann. We won't let it.'"

He went silent, and she looked over at him. He wore a frown.

"How?" he said quietly. "How do you not let the darkness consume you?"

Oh. "My mom's way was truth. She said to me, 'Jo, even though life feels out of control, it's not, and we're going to hold on to truth.' She's a strong Christian, and every time life felt overwhelming, she'd find a Bible verse and paste it on our cabinets or the walls or the refrigerator—even the bathroom mirror. Our house was full of God's word. I couldn't escape it." She closed her eyes. "'Where can I go from your spirit? Where can I flee from your presence? If I say, "Surely the darkness will hide me and the light become night around me," even the darkness will not be dark to you; the night will shine like the day, for darkness is as light to you.'"

She opened her eyes, Crew's gaze still fixed on her. Then, slowly, he nodded.

"I know that verse. My father became a Christian in prison. Took me to the prison Bible study. I accepted Jesus as my Savior but . . ." He blew a breath. "Maybe I've forgotten that a little."

"Not anymore." She got up, walked over to

him, knelt next to him. His eyes widened, but she just took his hand. "'Two are better than one. Though one may be overpowered, two can defend themselves. A cord of three strands is not quickly broken.'"

"There's something in that verse about keeping warm," he said. "'How can one keep warm alone?'"

Oh.

Then he winked and grinned. "Just kidding there, Wolf Girl. You're safe with me." He squeezed her hand, then let go. "Go to bed. Sleep. I promise, I won't try and kiss you again."

And as she lay down, wrapped the blanket around her, she closed her eyes.

Bummer. She might not mind being kissed again.

FIVE

THE LONGER THEY STAYED, THE LESS he could protect her. Because as much as Crew meant what he'd said, he might not be a match for the rabble who could hurt her.

Starting with Jer.

He'd seen how the big man had looked at her when Crew had led her away to the guest cabin last night. And then later, when he sat outside the shower room, Jer had come out of the bunkhouse, sat on the porch, smoking a cigarette, the ember like an eye glowing in the night.

Crew needed to get her away as soon as he could.

Which started with a conversation with Viper.

He didn't even like leaving her alone in the

cabin, sound asleep, the sun casting across her in the room through the grimy window, illuminating deep copper strands in her now-dry hair. She slept sweetly, her face on her hands, covered in the blanket, and he refused to let himself watch her and instead, locked the door behind him, the key in his pocket, and headed to Viper's office.

The smell of eggs and bacon sizzling on the griddle filled the hall as he entered. They'd brought in a side of pork and received eggs from a nearby homestead, who clearly had no idea who they'd dealt with.

Then again, Viper kept a lid on their true purpose, just one of many groups who hid out in the Alaskan forest. Some of them for religious reasons, others hippie or art communes, others simply survival communities.

He knocked on Viper's closed office door, heard steps inside, and Viper stood in the opening. He wore a black canvas jacket, his meaty hand on the frame as he considered Crew. Then he opened the door. Motioned with his head.

Crew stepped inside. Didn't glance at the table with the maps. No need to raise suspicion. However, he did spot her backpack in the office. "I have a plan."

Viper folded his arms across his barrel chest, his legs planted. "For what?"

"You want to get the smokejumpers for torching our camp, right?"

The explosion played in Viper's dark eyes. "I'm listening."

"Let me take her back to her camp. Hang around with her people until they get another callout. I'll come back with the coordinates, you—we—can take them out while they're focused on a fire."

A deep breath, as if Viper might be considering his words. "She tell you where they found her?"

Crew shook his head.

"What was she doing out here?" He walked to the window, stared out. It overlooked the guest cabin.

"She was fighting a fire. Went looking for a den of pups she's been trying to locate. She's working on her master's thesis on the local wolf population."

Lying rule number one—stick to the truth as much as possible.

He said nothing.

"I told you about the wolf, right? The dead one? It was one she was tracking. That's how we met. I helped her dispose of the body. We hit it off."

"That's why you got back late?" Viper turned, wore a hint of a smile. "I thought you'd left some things out."

Crew shrugged, added a grin. "I realized she was with the smokejumpers. Thought maybe I'd use that to find them." He lifted a shoulder. "Didn't mean I didn't enjoy it."

Viper laughed.

Crew's gut tightened. "I think she just got lost, boss. She's not a threat."

More silence.

"Okay. Twenty-four hours. You're not back then with an update, I send Jer to find you." He motioned with his head. "Get out of here."

Crew pointed to the pack. "Can I take that?"

Viper nodded. "Nothing but food and equipment in it. But we're keeping the radio." He gestured to the small handheld on the desk, on top of all the maps.

"Yes, sir." He grabbed the pack, then backed out of the room, keeping it easy, trying not to sprint back to the cabin. He even picked up a plate of eggs and bacon on his way through.

Not worried.

But his chest loosened a little when he reached the still-locked door.

However, inside, JoJo was up, pacing. "You locked me in here?" She'd changed back into her canvas pants, probably because the pair he'd given her had nearly fallen from her hips, dragged on the floor.

He set down the eggs, the pack over his shoulder. "I locked the guys *out*."

"Oh." She looked at the eggs. "Thanks."

"Eat. We're leaving."

She sat down and dug into breakfast. He couldn't eat, not with the clench inside. Instead, he stood at the window.

"You're really jumpy."

He glanced over his shoulder at her. "There's this guy named Jer who is . . . dangerous. He was watching you last night, and I didn't see him this morning, and that gives me the willies. He's connected somehow to something bigger. He disappeared for a year and then just waltzed back into camp, no big deal." He turned. "Ready?"

She had finished most of the plate. "Yeah. That my pack?"

He swung it onto the floor. "They kept your radio."

"I still have my phone."

He raised an eyebrow.

"I tucked it into my waistband pouch when I heard the ATVs." She indicated a space in her waistband.

"Smart. Okay, so here's the deal. We need to get you back to the jump base."

"Not without finding the pups."

He stared at her. "Have you lost your mind? The longer we hang out in SOR territory, the more they get suspicious. I barely got Viper to let you leave."

She picked up her pack, strapped it on. "How did you get him to let me leave?"

Oh. And he didn't want to tell her, but, shoot. He was tired of lying. He cut his voice low. "I told him that I'd come back with information about how to ambush your team."

She froze, stared at him.

"Never would I do that, JoJo. But I had to tell him something believable."

She swallowed, her mouth tight, what looked like wariness in her eyes.

Shoot. "Fine. We'll track down the pups if we can. And then we're done with this game. You're going back to safety."

"Okay."

He reached for the doorknob. "And on the way, you show me that greenhouse."

She nodded.

Ghost, a guy in his mid-twenties, an ex-military bearing about him, guarded the vehicle shed.

"Security sweep," Crew said.

Ghost glanced at JoJo. "And her?"

He cut his voice low. "Viper told me to get rid of her."

Ghost just nodded.

Oh, he hated these people.

He commandeered a truck, and JoJo climbed in the passenger side. Security let him through the gate, the guys eyeing him. But he'd invested over twelve dark months of his life earning trust. Time to cash it in.

He gunned it away from the enclave, down a rutted road. "Where's the pups' den?"

"I need a map."

"Glove compartment."

She opened it and spread out the topographical map. Found the dirt road that led along the Copper River, ran her finger up it, then west along a tributary that fed into the river. "I think it's around here."

"And the greenhouse?"

"Here." She pointed to an area south of the

river, maybe two clicks north. "Looks like a dirt road leads to it from this one."

"Could be an old homestead," he said. "Let's keep an eye out for the road."

The sky had turned a deep cerulean blue, the clouds high, the forest lush and green—a beautiful day in Alaska.

Or maybe he had simply, ever so briefly, escaped the darkness that clung to him back at the SOR compound.

"There's a road. It looks like it might be the one." She pointed to an indent in the woods, a bare, two-wheel track that looked suitable for an ATV but maybe not his truck. Still. "Let's try it."

He eased the truck onto the road, fir brushing the windows as he drove down the grassy path. The tree branches squealed against the truck, and JoJo braced her feet and hands on the dash and floorboard.

He laughed. "We'll make it."

"I know. It's a reflex. Sort of like right before I jump out of a plane. I brace myself."

"What made you want to be a smokejumper?"

They rounded a bend, and ahead, he spotted a clearing.

"My uncle was a smokejumper. And my cousin, Hannah. My mom would send me to visit them during the summers, a little town called Ember, where the entire town fights fire. I got fire fever, joined the local hotshot team when I was eighteen, and have been a little addicted ever since."

Yes, a cabin, the roof sprouting grass and even a little tree. He pulled into the yard.

"So why don't you just go full-time firefighter instead of chasing wolves?"

She reached for the handle. "My dad, I guess. And of course, there's the fear that someday I'll end up face down in a shake-and-bake, being burned to death." She got out.

He sat there. What?

But his gaze fixed on a Quonset hut in a clearing on the property. A trail led to it, evidence of at least recent activity.

He got out and followed her. She had already opened the door.

Inside, the place sweated with humidity, water sprayers misting on the plants, sunlight drab but filtering in upon row after row of flowering nightshade.

"This is . . ."

"Lethal," she said. Looked at him, her mouth tight.

"Let's get out of here. Because if the SOR runs

this place, there is probably security. The last thing we need is to get caught poking around."

He shut the door.

She put a hand on his arm. "Too late, I think." She pointed to a nearby tree.

And in that tree, a camera.

Perfect. "Let's go," he said. "We're running out of time."

Maybe she shouldn't have made Crew stop to look for the pups.

Maybe JoJo should have heeded the look in his eyes, the one that'd flashed fear a second before he'd gotten into the truck, turned around in the yard, and floored it—well, as fast he could given the narrow drive—to the dirt road.

He'd clenched his jaw so tight she thought he might break molars. Drove in silence all the way until they reached the dirt road.

And then, instead of turning south to Copper Mountain, he'd headed north.

To the place where she'd supposed the pups' den might be.

Because apparently, Crew, who harbored secrets, was also a promise keeper.

Now, they stood on a bluff overlooking the

tributary—more of a creek that tore through the rock and valley, curling around a hillside and gaining froth and speed as it hit the main river. But here, it seemed to meander, the area secluded and possibly perfect for a wolf's den.

Please, God.

And maybe her words from last night had found her, wrapped around her heart, because she'd woken with her mother's voice in her head.

Or maybe God's voice. *So do not fear, for I am with you. I will strengthen you and help you.*

Funny, she used to wake up often with a verse in her head. She couldn't remember the last time, however.

"Do you see anything?" Crew, standing behind her, his scent raking off him, mingling with the wind, stirring inside her.

She'd watched him sleep last night, just for a moment, his dark lashes whispering against his cheekbones, his a sort of restlessness even in his repose.

They mess with you, they mess with me.

"I don't know. We might need to get closer to the river, see if we can find some scat. Wait—" Her view stopped on carrion near the water's edge. Dark gray fur . . . oh no. "I think I found Cleo."

She handed him the monocular. "By the water, next to that trio of birch trees."

She moved the monocular for him.

"Yeah, I see it."

"Can we get down there?"

He lowered the glass. "Let's go." Then he held out his hand.

She took it, held on. *Two are better than one.*

He led her down the slope, grabbing on to tree limbs, bracing his feet on rocks, tiny pebbles shooting down before them. Her own personal Pulaski.

They reached the flatter terrain, worked their way to the creek bank, and she let go when she spotted the carcass. Flies lifted from the remains, and she covered her nose with her handkerchief, kneeling by the body. "Yeah, it's Cleo. She still has her tracking collar. It seems she hasn't been dead for long. Not a lot of decay. And she wasn't attacked. No blood."

"Disease?"

"Maybe." She stood up. "Hopefully the pups are still alive. I don't think she'd go far from them, especially without Brutus to protect them. But where's the pack?" She studied the shoreline opposite the creek bed. Rocky, with shallow overhangs and caves.

"Maybe they got scared off. Dogs can smell death and disease, so . . . Although, if she ate poisoned fish, wouldn't she have smelled it?"

She nodded, started walking down the riverbank. "Unless it smelled like something she might be familiar with . . . like nightshade."

"Do wolves eat dead fish?"

"If prey is scarce. They're predators, but they're also scavengers." She'd stopped, seeing another mound of fur farther up the shore. "Oh no."

He followed her and confirmed her fears as they came closer. "It looks like a pup."

"Yeah." She knelt beside this one too. Not as many flies. "He looks more recent."

Crew put a hand on her shoulder. "Hear that?"

She stood, listened over the rush of the creek. A tiny, high-pitched moan. "Whining."

"Hungry puppies?"

She studied the creek, searching the rock.

"There," he said, pointing upstream. "See the pup?"

Indeed, a gray mound of fur lay on the stream bed, outside the mouth of a recess.

She ran down the riverbed, toward the animal. The creek here ran maybe a foot or two deep, and she splashed out, nearly fell save for Crew's hand on her elbow, and then she almost pulled him down.

He hooked her hand, steadied her as she crossed the deepest part and over to the other side.

The pup lay as if sleeping but didn't raise its head, the wind raking through the fur. She knelt and put her hand on its body.

No breath.

Crew splashed up behind her. "Is it alive?"

"No."

He moved past her, toward the cave, leaned in. "There are two more in here. They look weak, but at least one is alive."

She stood up in time for him to haul out a pup, maybe twenty pounds, whining but lethargic. He passed it over to her. The animal burrowed into her.

He retrieved the next one, also lethargic. "What's wrong with them?"

"Mama might have brought home the diseased fish." She ran her hand over the pup's fur. "They'll die if we don't get them into the vet."

He had the other tucked in his arm. "Let's go."

She ventured out again across the river, Crew behind her, and then started off in a jog toward the truck, maybe a mile away, cross-country.

Crew kept up with her, which said something about his fitness, because she'd been training all summer—running, hauling equipment, climbing mountains, digging trenches.

Then again, who knew what he did in the lair of evil? She didn't want to think about it. But even as she slowed, still fast-walking, his story about prison came back to her.

"So, are you working for the FBI?"

He looked at her, frowned. "Yes. But I'm not an agent, thanks to the felony. Paid informant. I don't love the term, but it's all I got."

"I like Lumberjack Batman."

He grinned. Shook his head.

"So if you get caught up in whatever they're doing, do you get arrested? Go back to jail?"

His smile dimmed, and he pointed to a trail. "Not if Rio gets there first. But . . . I hope not."

Felt like he should have more reassurances than that. But she said nothing as he picked up his pace again, his feet thumping along the deer trail.

She kept up, the pup moaning now and again.

They reached the truck, the sun high, and he took the pups as she got into the passenger side, then handed them to her. "Buckle in." They lay, their heads on her lap, barely breathing.

He climbed in. "Where to?"

"There's a vet office in town. Let's start there. I'll call Peyton and ask her to meet us."

Cell signal didn't hit until five miles down the road, but she got ahold of Peyton's voicemail and left an update.

Twenty minutes later, they pulled into town, and she directed him past Main Street, a little way past town, south, to the vet she'd seen on her drive to Copper Mountain.

They pulled up into the gravel lot of the clinic. Crew got out and opened the passenger door, pulled out a puppy.

A woman with long black hair, wearing a thermal shirt and khakis, met them at the door. "Can I help you?"

"We're looking for the vet," Crew said.

"That's me. My name is Anuk."

It was a simple office with a waiting room and a hallway to the back. A bigger man appeared, large and blond. "What's going on?"

JoJo lifted the puppy. "These are wolf pups. We think their parents were poisoned, and we think these guys ate the same fish. They're the only ones in the litter left."

Anuk took the wolf from JoJo. "Gunnar, can you get the other?"

The big man came over to Crew, took the animal.

JoJo followed them back into an exam room with a stainless-steel table. Anuk put the pup down. It lay there, and she pulled out a stethoscope, listened, then tested its pulse. Breathing. "Let's get them into oxygen cages, and then I'll draw some blood."

Gunnar picked up his pup and carried it out of the room.

Anuk turned to them. "I'll let you know what I find out. Is there a number I can call?"

"I'm not leaving them," JoJo said.

"Jo," Crew said quietly. "Let's get you back to your base."

She rounded on him, ready to—

What? He stood there, his gaze in hers, frowning, clearly worried. And maybe not just about the dogs.

And probably she looked as frayed as she felt, still grimy, still buzzing a little from the last twenty-four hours—the fire, the kidnapping, the pups . . .

Girlfriend.

Except she wasn't the girlfriend anymore, right?

"Give her your number, Jo," he said softly, touching her hand. Squeezing.

She didn't know what to think. "Okay."

While Gunnar retrieved the other dog, she left her contact information—and Peyton's—with Anuk.

Then she climbed back into the truck, her bones suddenly turning to liquid.

He joined her. "You okay?"

"I don't know. Maybe we should stop in town on the way and talk to Peyton. And then I should probably check in with the base."

"I'm surprised they haven't sent out a search party. Your buddy *Hammer*."

She looked at him, grinned. "Hammer is just a friend." And then her eyes widened. What? What did she just say? Oh . . . no . . . "Not that it matters."

He eyed her, then turned back. "Right. Not that it matters."

She leaned back, closed her eyes. Not that it mattered at all.

But as he pulled out and drove north, as he hummed along to a country song that came on the radio, his voice a deep tenor, thrumming through her, as she recalled Crew holding on to the wolf pup, fighting to save its life, she sort of wanted it to matter, very, very much.

SIX

TRUTH WAS, HE DIDN'T WANT TO RE-
turn to the SOR camp. Crew stood outside the
National Park Service office, leaning against
his truck, hands in his pockets, fighting the urge to
just ... keep driving.

Okay, yes, he'd meet with Rio first and deliver
the information about the nightshade garden and
his suspicion that it was used in the bioweapon
the SOR was manufacturing.

And then ... keep driving.

Aw, to where, exactly? Because he had to bring
JoJo back to the fire crew base. He couldn't just
drive into the sunset with a woman he'd only
known for twenty-four hours.

Right?

"Okay, Peyton will check on the pups. I'm ready to go."

JoJo came down the steps, still dressed in his flannel shirt, her hair in a fresh braid, wearing her sooty pants, a smile on her face that seemed a thousand watts brighter than when they'd left the vet's office.

"Peyton have good news?"

"Just that she located the pack and that they seemed to all be on the move. She thinks they've found new alphas and abandoned Cleo and Brutus after their deaths."

"And that's a good thing?" He leaned up from the truck.

"It means that maybe they've moved on from the death zone."

He'd like to move on from the death zone. He turned to unlock his door when he spotted—seriously? His handler seemed to have radar on him.

Okay, not fair since he'd texted Rio and told him he was in town. Except Rio didn't seem to notice him as he crossed the street, headed for the sheriff's office.

Crew pocketed his keys. "How about some dinner?"

JoJo stood at her passenger door. Considered

him. "That smoke from the Midnight Sun Saloon does smell amazing."

He'd spent the better part of twenty minutes consuming that smell—barbecue, garlic, and smoky ribs from the smoker. He'd eaten there a few times over the past year, and now his stomach gurgled. "Let's walk down there."

She came back around, glanced at him. "Are you stalling?"

"Me? What?" And he even had the crazy urge to hold out his hand for her to take.

Nope. Too weird. They weren't dating. Not really. And she might see people she knew here.

And it hit him then that anyone who saw him here knew him as an SOR member. So wasn't that awesome.

He stuck his hands in his pockets, headed down the street, past the outfitters store, the sports store, the hardware store, the coffee shop. At the sheriff's office, he slowed, glanced in through the glass.

Rio stood talking with Sheriff Deke Starr, who knew exactly what Crew might be up to, so . . . "Go get us seats. I'm going to talk to the sheriff."

She eyed him. "Really?"

"He knows. And Rio is in there. But . . . just go, okay?"

She frowned but nodded.

And he hated that maybe she thought he might be lying. But frankly, he didn't want Rio asking questions about why he was with JoJo . . . *again*.

In Rio's eyes—and maybe his own—he was still a criminal. A felon.

Probably not someone who should be with a woman like JoJo. And that truth sat like a boulder in his gut as he waited until she crossed the street, then headed inside.

Rio glance at him. Frowned.

"I found the source of the poison," Crew said, walking up to him. He glanced at Deke, who also frowned.

He'd met Deke. Liked him, but he never felt super comfortable around law enforcement. At least, not after his arrest.

Maybe it was in his head.

"What poison?" Deke said.

"We think the SOR is creating a bioweapon," Rio said. He glanced out the window, then headed to a conference room.

Crew followed, and Deke shut the door behind him.

"You're taking a big risk, Crew," Rio said. "You should be in camp."

"It's a long story—but I found a greenhouse

filled with nightshade berry plants. I think it's what killed the salmon and the wolves."

"You think they're using the nightshade to create the bioweapon?" Rio said.

"Part of it. It causes hallucinations and delirium, can lead to death, so . . ." He turned to the map of the area tacked on the wall. Ran his finger up the Copper River to the tributary, then west until he found the dirt road with the homestead. "Here. It's right here."

"That's the old Hamilton place," said Deke. "They left a few years ago after Gareth Hamilton was killed in a hunting accident."

Crew didn't want to suggest that maybe it hadn't been an accident.

"Any luck on finding the warehouse where they're storing this?" Again, Rio.

"No. I looked for a map in Viper's office, but I nearly got caught."

Rio nodded.

And he let the silence fill in the rest.

"Are they onto you, Crew?" This from Deke.

Rio's mouth tightened.

Crew shook his head. "I don't think so. But I did hear them talking. They're expecting someone. Viper called him 'the big guy,' so . . ."

"When?" Rio said.

"In the next few days."

He looked away, at the map. Then at the wall, filled with current BOLO pictures and the FBI top-ten list. Stilled. Took a step toward the list and the pictures next to the names and descriptions of the wanted. A man, dark hair, a scar under his eye, bearded. "That's Viper."

Rio stepped up next to him. "You sure?"

"Pretty sure. Same scar. Same eyes." He turned to Rio. "Can't we just bring him in, lean on him . . ." And he didn't want to sound tired or wrung out or—

Rio touched his shoulder. "Give us until the big guy comes in. And then, if you haven't figured out the warehouse yet, we'll grab Viper, pull you out, okay?"

Crew swallowed. Nodded. Sighed. "I gotta go."

"Out the back," Deke said. He motioned to the door at the back of the room.

Crew headed for it.

"Crew," Rio said. "Stay the course."

He nodded and stepped outside. Headed around the building, then down the row of parking lots, and finally emerged on the other side of the Last Frontier Bakery.

Jogged across the street.

Not a lot of cars at the Midnight Sun Saloon,

and he entered to music from the jukebox and a few patrons at the long bar nursing sodas or baskets of fries.

JoJo sat in a red vinyl booth, looking at a menu. She waved at him as if he couldn't see her like a beacon, drawing him to herself.

He slid into the booth opposite her. "Hey."

"I ordered you a root beer. And a basket of fries."

"I could kiss you."

Her eyes widened.

Oh. His did too. "Sorry. I, uh . . ."

She laughed then. "Still undercover?"

Please, yes. "Maybe. Hard not to look over my shoulder every second."

She set down the menu as a waitress came over, delivered their sodas. "Fries are on their way. What'll ya have?"

They ordered ribs, and he appreciated a girl with an appetite.

"So, is this your first 'undercover' gig?" She finger quoted the word. The music covered up her voice.

"No. I embedded into a motorcycle gang in Anchorage, helped Rio take down some drug smugglers."

"So you two are partners."

"I wouldn't say that. I owe Rio a lot."

"Feels like he owes you a lot." She took a sip of her soda. Raised an eyebrow.

Huh, he'd never thought of it that way.

"Well, maybe after this, I'm done."

The waitress delivered the fries. JoJo took one. "Delish. And why?"

He sighed. "I don't know. I really want to get into law enforcement—work for the DEA or maybe the local police. But my felony record disqualifies me. I thought about the military, but I'd have to get a waiver. It feels like this is my only option, but . . ." He shook his head.

"Tired of hanging out with evil."

He looked at her, nodded. Sighed. "When my dad came back from Iraq, it was . . . well, my mom was so happy, and he got discharged, and we rented this house outside Anchorage, and I had a dog, and he worked as a car mechanic for a while. It was good."

"Is that where you learned how to hot-wire cars?"

She said it without judgment, just a question, and it didn't hurt.

"And overhaul engines. I can replace a head gasket, even rebuild a transmission in record time. I was planning on being a mechanic when I . . .

Anyway. I'm not sure I can go back to that either, given my record."

She nodded. "What do you want to do?"

He looked up. Met her eyes. "Something that matters."

She held his gaze, nodded, then reached out and touched his hand. Softly, then with a firmer grip. "You do, Crew. You do."

He stared at her and then turned his hand around and threaded her fingers through his. Squeezed.

Met her eyes. Wow, he wanted to hold on to her. And the urge to run swept through him again.

"I thought that was you."

He stilled, looked up, and everything inside him emptied.

Jer stood at the table, hands in his pockets, looking at him, then back to JoJo.

And he knew, right then, he had to change his answer to Deke's question.

Yes. Yes, they were onto him.

She could nearly feel his worry radiating off him as Crew drove her north, to the Midnight Sun base.

The Styrofoam container with leftover ribs

sat between them on the seat, and she rested her hand on it, but what she really wanted to do was take his hand again.

Return to that moment when the thug named Jer had shown up at their table and the spooked expression had flashed through Crew's heart-breaking eyes.

Then it'd vanished behind a wall of darkness, and he'd gone all silent and remote on her.

Practically wolfed down the ribs, not looking at her.

Jer had taken a position at a nearby table, barbecue sauce layering his beard, and oh, she couldn't look at him without her gut turning. And it wasn't just his eating habits.

The man had smiled at Crew, something of smug satisfaction, and she just couldn't shake it off.

"How much trouble are you in?" she said.

Crew looked over at her. Back to the road. "None, probably, since Jer caught me holding your hand. Cover intact."

"Really? Because it didn't feel that way."

He sighed. "The disturbing part is that he probably got sent to town to find me. Track me. Which means Viper didn't buy our girl-friend-boyfriend bit."

"Maybe you should have kissed me again." Yes, she'd said that, and she didn't care.

"Maybe," he said, but a small smile eked up his face.

Attaboy.

"I don't think you should go back, Crew. It's too dangerous."

They'd traveled out of town, the base just up ahead, and the closer they got, the more her stomach clenched. She wasn't falling for him—she just . . . cared, was all.

Lumberjack Batman just kept on saving her life and, well, who wouldn't care?

"I have to go back. Not only do I need to find where they're making and storing this biohazard they're synthesizing with the nightshade, but we suspect they're funded by big bucks. And according to a conversation I just heard, those big bucks might be showing up in a few days. Rio wants me to stick around and find out who."

"Rio isn't the one who is going to get beat up and tortured if he's found out!" Oh, whoops.

Crew touched the brakes, slowed, then pulled over. Turned to her. Shoot, she was crying a little, probably just tired.

"Jo—"

"I'm fine." She turned to him. "It's none of my business."

"As my current girlfriend, it's sort of your business." He seemed to start to reach out, touch her cheek, then stopped.

Shoot.

What—

"As your *former* girlfriend, I really don't want you going back there. We can figure out another way to get these guys."

"We?"

"Two are better than one. Maybe..." She drew in a breath, and yes, that was it. "I should go back with you—"

"Have you lost your mind?" Now he was shouting.

She didn't flinch, just folded her arms. "If they think we're dating, then they'll let me back in. I can help."

"What? Distract Viper while I search the camp?"

"Maybe."

"I might be sick. I was *kidding*. And never mind what Jer has on his brain—no, it's not even a topic of conversation." He turned back and put the truck in Drive.

"Crew!"

"You have a job, JoJo. One, if I am correct, you're AWOL from." He shook his head over and over as he drove.

She touched his arm. "Calm down, Crew."

He glanced at her, molars tight again.

"Okay. I get it. But I just . . . I can't but feel like if you go back there"—and her stupid eyes filled again—"you'll get killed."

He drew in a breath, his mouth tightening into a grim line. "Maybe that's all a guy like me has to look forward to."

"What?"

He shook his head again and turned onto the dirt road leading to the base.

"Crew—"

"I don't want to talk about it. Where do I drop you?"

She turned back, folded her arms, her shoulders rising and falling with her breaths. "Up here, at the administrative building. I need to check in."

They drove up the dirt road, the grass mowed on either side—the handiwork of one of their dispatchers who hated being indoors.

Cutting through the middle of the camp, a runway held a couple jump planes waiting for action and a chopper. A number of Quonsets sat on the other side of the runway, by the vehicle depots and the chopper pads, along with the mess hall and the hangar, which held equipment and attached to their parachute bay.

Cabins and RV parking lined up along the road, a firepit in the center. As he pulled into the parking lot in front of the admin building, JoJo spotted Tori walking from the building to the women's cabin. A couple hotshots sat on the porch steps of the men's cabin.

"A lot different from the SOR base. We had something like this before you guys blew it up."

She looked at him. "Us guys?"

"I didn't meant it that way. But it was less . . . rustic. After it was . . . blown up . . . the SOR scattered."

"How many more compounds are there?"

"I don't know. Which is why I need to go back, JoJo."

And they were back to that.

He parked and she got out, held the door open. "Come in. Meet Tucker."

He glanced over at her. "Why?"

"So if we have to blow up one of your compounds again, he knows you're one of the good guys."

His mouth opened. And she didn't know where that'd come from, but—"Sorry."

But he blinked at her.

And then he put the truck into Park, turned it off, and got out.

Came around.

"Really?"

"I need to bring back something for Viper. He thinks I'm going to get information on where you're jumping next. Might be good if I knew where *not* to send him."

"Hard to say since we don't know where a fire might start. But we do have some priority management areas where, if there is a fire, we'll definitely drop in."

She held the door open for him.

Inside, the building was spare, a few wooden walls to divide the spaces, humming with the voices of dispatchers and other personnel. She walked upstairs to Tucker Newman's office and knocked on the half-open door.

Inside, Tucker—tall, brown hair, dressed in green pants and a white shirt—turned. "JoJo?"

"Hey, Chief. I just wanted to let Jade know I'm back."

"She's on her day off, but I'll let her know." His gaze trekked past her to Crew.

Jo turned. "This is Crew. He lives out in the

backcountry. He picked me up and brought me back."

Tucker reached out for Crew's hand. "Thanks for bringing in one of our jumpers."

Crew shook it, but his gaze was on a giant map on the wall with tacks marking recent fires. He stepped into the office. "Are these active fires?"

"Yes. The green are limited management fires, the orange are fires we're watching. The red, of course, are active, but we've gotten control of those."

"So the green are areas of fire but no personnel deployed?"

"Land management wants to let ecology take its course. Not every fire needs to be stopped. It'll burn itself out eventually. We need to manage the ones that could cost homes and lives."

Crew nodded, glanced at JoJo, gave her a tight smile.

She smiled back, her throat thick. Apparently, he'd gotten what he needed.

"Thanks."

Right then, something in Crew's face changed. His breathing quickened.

"Oh my gosh, it's *you*."

JoJo turned. Jamie Winters had walked up behind her. She stared at Crew. "You were at the compound."

He looked at JoJo. Back to Jamie. "Um . . ." He cut his voice low. "Yeah. Uh . . . can we talk in the hall?"

Jamie's eyes widened, and Crew all but pushed her into the hallway and into a nearby room.

JoJo followed, heard him ask, "Are you okay?"

What?

Jamie nodded. "Yeah. What are you doing here?"

"Long story."

"Have you seen Tristan?"

Tristan? Oh, right—Jamie's brother.

Crew looked a little stricken. "Is he missing?"

Jamie nodded. "He was almost murdered. Went AWOL from the hospital."

He hung a hand behind his neck. Shook his head. "Wow. No, I haven't."

"Excuse me, who is this?" Tucker had come up behind them.

Jamie turned. "It's okay, Tucker. He's not with the SOR. He was at the compound. Helped Logan and me escape."

The realization punched JoJo. Oh no. She'd blown his cover bringing him here. *Sorry, Crew.*

"Long story," Crew said to Tucker. He turned

back to Jamie. "I'll keep my eye out and let you know if I hear anything." He reached out and touched her arm. "But he's smart. And capable. I'm sure he's okay."

"Thanks." Jamie lifted her tablet. "But I have a question. I saw a map in the office when I met with your leader, and I recreated it." She seemed to be pulling it up and now turned the tablet toward him. "Do you recognize it?"

He stared at the tablet, then up at the map on the wall. Back to the tablet. "Can you print this for me?"

"Sure."

A moment later, the printer spat out the print, full color. He picked it up, studied it again.

Jamie looked over his shoulder. "The only thing I recognize is the Refuge, a community the team evacuated in the path of a fire. Oh, and your compound." She pointed to two markers. "They were marked on the map, along with these others. I colored them in according to what I remember. Black, green, yellow."

"Good memory." He folded the paper. Looked at Jo. "I need to go."

Right. She looked away.

"Thanks," he said to Jamie, then Tucker. Then he walked past her.

But he hooked her hand on the way. And shoot, if she didn't hold on.

He brought her out of the front doors, then around the side of the building, away from the cabins and the mess hall. Just the administrative building to her back, the faraway hills behind him, a few planes and hangars, quiet under the blue sky.

Her heart banged as she looked up at him into his dark eyes, the way they held her. "What?"

"This is a map of all the SOR compounds."

"What?"

"I'm not sure what the other places are but . . . maybe the warehouse is on this map."

She put a hand to his chest, his heart banging against it. "So you can find it?"

"Maybe. Hopefully."

"And then get out."

He nodded.

And then come back to me. And she didn't say it—or maybe not—but she thought it, and maybe . . . aw, maybe he saw it in her eyes.

Because his gaze dropped to her mouth, back to her eyes, and he swallowed, and she just couldn't stop herself.

She put her hands on him, pulled herself up, and kissed him.

And maybe he'd seen her intention in her eyes, maybe anticipated it, because he was right there, meeting her halfway.

All in.

He put a hand on the wall behind her, the other around her waist, and pulled her against himself, even as she slid her arms around his neck.

All in.

She kissed him like a girlfriend, like she knew him, tasting him, wanting him, as if they had a past and a future, but also as if right now might be everything.

The only thing.

He stepped up to her, both arms around her now, and she let herself hold on to him, let him take control.

Let herself go.

He emitted a tiny groan, but she didn't let him pull away. Tightened her hold on him, urging him to deepen his kiss, and letting him.

He was rescue and danger, safety and recklessness, secrets and vulnerability. And he tasted like the woods, of the world she wanted to inhabit.

Don't go.

But she couldn't hold on to him. Not when she had to come up for breath and he met her eyes. "You're making this difficult."

"I hope so."

He touched his forehead to hers. Took a breath.

"I knew you wanted to kiss me again." She wasn't sure why she said that, but something simply nudged her to reach out, push at the darkness in his eyes.

He smiled at her, shook his head. "Listen. Stay alive. This isn't over yet."

"No, it's not. Please . . . come back to me."

He said nothing, so much in his expression, tight, fierce. Then he let her go, just like that, leaving her shaking, a little broken, as he walked out to his truck.

And drove back to the den of iniquity.

SEVEN

HOW COULD SHE MISS SO MUCH A guy she barely knew?

Okay, she knew Crew a lot more than guys she'd worked with for two years. Like for example Hammer, who'd surprised her the night she got back by sitting down at the mess hall and asking her if she'd found her baby wolves.

She'd barely heard the man speak a full sentence in two years, so, yeah. But she had worked with him, knew he was a guy she could count on.

But she knew Crew's dreams, his fears, his hopes.

And for the life of her couldn't erase from her brain, her lips, the touch of him as he'd kissed her.

Yeah, she knew him, enough to know why she'd

stared at the ceiling, tossing the last three nights away.

Her heart just couldn't stop conjuring up the terrible things that Viper or Jer might be doing to him.

Which was why she'd rolled out of bed at— well, it couldn't rightly be called dawn, not with the sun already blazing, but early enough to see the mess hall closed, not even coffee perking. So she'd taken a run down the dirt road, all the way to the concrete drive and then down a ways, enough so that the smells of the forest could clear the fog from her brain, renew her spirit.

Because of the Lord's great love we are not consumed, for his compassions never fail. They are new every morning; great is your faithfulness.

Yes. Truth. She breathed it in as she turned and ran back.

Please, God, help Crew to see Your faithfulness. Deliver him from evil.

Her feet slapped the dirt, her breaths hard as she rounded back onto the drive.

But those who hope in the Lord will renew their strength. They will soar on wings like eagles; they will run and not grow weary, they will walk and not be faint.

Yes. *Please, God, help him to not grow weary . . .*

Footsteps sounded behind her, and she jerked around.

Hammer came up, huffing hard, sweat rolling out of his dark-blond hair. He had a military bearing, a military build, all hard planes and thick arms, strong legs. He wore a pair of compression shorts and a T-shirt, glanced at her. "Hey."

She kept running. "Hey."

He fell in beside her. "You should take someone with you when you go running. Bears."

She glanced at him. "You're not afraid of bears?"

He smiled at her. "I am the bear."

She rolled her eyes. He gave a low chuckle. Weird, but okay.

They ran to the barracks, and she veered into hers, cooling down into a stretch at the steps, then headed inside.

Tori was up, already dressed, and Jamie's bunk was empty too as JoJo walked down to her room. Cadee came out of their space, drying her hair with a towel, wearing shorts and a T-shirt. "Hey, Jo, you got a call while you were out." She pointed to the cell phone on her bunk.

JoJo picked it up. Peyton. She dialed as she pulled off her shoes.

"Jo. Hey," Peyton said, and clinking sounded

in the ambient noise. So, probably at breakfast at her parents' B&B. "The pups survived. Anuk found an antidote that counteracted the poison, but yes, she traced it to nightshade in their systems, along with a few other substances. Salmon in their stomachs. She's sending them to a wildlife rehabilitation center in Anchorage. Good job."

"Thanks, Peyton." She sank onto her cot as she hung up.

"We're repacking chutes after breakfast." This from Tori, who was lacing up her boots. "But Jamie said she wanted to see you in her office, when you could."

"No fires?" She stood up, grabbing her towel.

"Antsy for a callout?" Cadee said, pulling on a sweatshirt.

Maybe. She couldn't put a finger on it, but . . .

Aw, who was she kidding? She was antsy to hear anything about Crew.

She showered, stopped in the mess hall, loaded up coffee in her insulated mug, then carried it over to Jamie's office.

The woman had sort of set up camp at the fire base. Apparently, she had taken Jade Ransom's idea about the tracker ring and manufactured them. And she was loaded—she'd purchased the team a new jump plane after theirs went down during the rescue to save Jamie's life. She also, apparently, ran a billion-dollar finance business. So what she was doing at the Midnight Sun base camp seemed . . .

Well, there was Logan of course.

And her missing brother.

So maybe it wasn't so strange to see the woman sitting on a molded vinyl chair at a folding table, staring at her laptop, charts and maps tacked to the wall of her cubicle.

She looked up when JoJo came in. "Hey." She got up and pointed to the map on the wall. "So, I did an overlay of the fire map and the map I showed Crew."

"The Sons of Revolution map?"

She nodded. "These three fires came from places marked in yellow on the SOR map." She pointed at yellow circles drawn around the places indicated in green on the fire map.

"Limited management areas."

"Yes. Places the FS wouldn't attribute to arson."

She took a sip of coffee. "You're saying they set those fires."

"I am."

"Do we have proof?"

"No." She stepped back. "But this one could be." She pointed to a yellow circle near a red pin.

"What's that?"

"The Refuge. That commune that Tori and Orion stayed in."

"Right. We helped them evacuate. I thought it was caused by lightning."

"Maybe. But maybe not. And I'm concerned about these places." She pointed to orange circles.

"No pushpins in those areas, so no fires there."

"No. But this is a small village, off-grid." She pointed to a dot inside the orange circle. "And this is a group of homesteaders, like the Refuge."

JoJo stared at the map, took another sip of coffee. "What are these red places? Wait—that's the compound that burned."

"Yes. We think these might be SOR encampments."

She counted. "Six."

"Including the one that burned. And they might not all be inhabited."

"And these blue circles?" She pointed to one north of the jump base, another deeper in the woods, northeast.

"Not sure."

Tucker knocked, then stuck his head in the office. "We have a callout on a fire on the north side of Chase. It's a small community about twenty clicks from here. We'll jump in to the north, send a team up from the south. Briefing in five."

She turned back to the map, stepped up to it.

Jamie had already pinpointed it. Small village, maybe five homes, so not even a village. Probably just a census center.

And no ring around it. Maybe just a random lightning strike, then.

She nodded and headed to the briefing room. The rest of her jump team had gathered, along with one of the hotshot crews. She took a seat next to Logan, lifted a fist. He bumped it.

Tucker, clearly taking over for Jade, stepped up to the board and ran through the fire, the plan of attack, and then assigned Skye as fire boss for the day. The fire hadn't yet reached Chase. Instead, it had started at a small camping area next to an inland lake. Hopefully uninhabited.

She headed to the gear room and kitted up, grabbed her helmet, and then jogged out to their Twin Otter. Hopped in beside Cadee, Tori, and Vince, Logan across from her. Hammer got in and settled beside Tori, now that Orion was nursing a dislocated shoulder. Those two had a thing going, evidenced by their companionship at meals, and she'd even spotted Orion walking Tori back to the women's barracks.

But fighting to survive together did that to people. *Two are better than one.*

She leaned her head back. *Please keep Crew safe, Lord.*

Skye jumped in along with Mark, Neil at the helm.

"Let's roll," Skye said and sat behind the pilot's seat, holding her helmet. She looked over at JoJo, gave her a thin-lipped smile.

What was that about? And then—wait. Skye's husband knew Crew. And it hit her then that Skye probably knew Crew. All that talk after she first met him, from Skye, about giving him a chance . . . Aw, too many secrets.

And now Skye looked away, as if holding more. Awesome.

The plane taxied, took off, leaving behind the fire base, ascending between the peaks, over the rich boreal forests, the meandering tributaries that fell into the mighty Copper River.

Ahead, the smallest trickle of smoke blotted the sky, dark gray, black at the center—fresh and burning hot—and it looked like it had found fuel other than woodlands.

The plane circled the fire, and JoJo glanced out the window. Yep, below them, in a large clearing, a barn burned. Probably filled with old tires, machinery, even gas tanks. A cabin stood not far away. Looked abandoned. Hopefully.

So, what—lightning strike on the barn? Felt off.

"There's a drop zone just east of here," said Mark. "Let's circle and I'll drop some ribbons."

Neil got them above the zone, and Mark and Skye tested the air, watched the wind, then Skye spooled them up.

"Wind's gusting just a little from the east. Might drive you northwest. Stay tight." She sent JoJo and Logan out on the first stick, and again, JoJo flew, losing herself in the majesty.

For as high as the heavens are above the earth, so great is his love for those who fear him.

Yes, she could lean into that.

She pulled her rip cord.

Waited for the tug of the chute to open, propel her up, catch the wind, stop her fall.

Nothing, and she looked up. The chute had deployed, but it twisted in the wind, tangled, the lines cluttering its deployment.

Logan floated high above her.

She bit back a word and felt for the cutaway. Released the primary chute, breathed out, and pulled the secondary.

The whoosh nearly stole her breath, the sudden unfurling halt and yank into the heavens. The harness cut into her thighs, the toggles spinning in the wind. She grabbed them, trying to steer.

The wind had already grabbed her, started to spin her.

She caught a glimpse of the fire to the west, the black smoke churning into the blue sky, the acrid scent burning her nose. Wrestling for control, she found Logan, already a half mile away, maybe, directing himself toward the drop zone.

Below her, forest rose, the black smoke roiled, and she was running out of time.

Well, she would just get to the fire sooner than her team. She angled toward the farm, the wide yard, and prayed the wind would be kind.

There was no going back now.

Crew sat on the stolen four-wheeler, watching the fire chew through the barn, the smoke burning his throat, the acrid odor stinging his nose.

But it was over. Please.

Longest four days of his life. He'd barely gotten out alive, really, and his next move would be to hightail it to Copper Mountain and warn Rio of what he'd seen.

The flames crested over the top of the barn,

breaking through the smoke, the sound a rumble, the fire popping, roaring.

Apparently, biohazard made for hot fuel.

Overhead, he spotted a plane, a red-and-white body, and he stilled. Aw, he'd seen a similar plane at the smokejumper base camp. No, no—

Yes.

There, in the sky, in the distance, tiny chutes unfurled. They drifted down, maybe a half mile away, plenty of distance between their drop zone and the barn.

They shouldn't have deployed. The barn sat away from the house a good fifty feet, and behind it, an old corral cordoned off the barn from the forest. A natural cut line.

He should go. Last thing he wanted was evidence that he'd started a fire. And while Rio might give him a high five, he'd have some explaining to do with the Forest Service. Especially if someone got hurt.

Please, God, no.

Funny, but he'd been praying a lot over the past few days, as if nudged from inside.

He stilled as he spotted a chute headed over the treetops, the jumper fighting with the toggles as the wind propelled him—oh no.

Toward the fire.

The jumper was falling fast, descending too quickly. No way would he clear the flames and fire of the barn.

Turn!

The wind of the fire seemed to catch the chute, then suck it into a spiral, and then the jumper disappeared into the smoke.

He stood up on the posts of the ATV, chest tight, searching.

Nothing.

Please, no—

Still no jumper. He sat down and gunned the ATV toward the fire, heading into the smoke as it funneled out of broken windows, the front door.

What if the fire had sucked him in?

What if it wasn't a him but—JoJo. Oh no . . . no . . .

He sped down the length of the building, smoke fighting through the roof, flickering out of windows. It was nearly impossible to see in the haze of the fire.

And then he spotted it—the chute, hung up on the weathervane of the barn, still at the apex, near the back. Ripped and now burning, the lines fluttering in the wind.

Please—

He rounded the back, shooting through the

corral, and there, on the backside of the barn, the jumper struggled, cutting the chute strings, hanging some twenty feet from the ground. But their pack was clipped on the haymow hook, the old pully system rusty and broken.

Fire burst from a nearby window.

Crew pulled up, leaped off the ATV.

The jumper had cut their strings, now fought the harness, the pack imprisoning them against the burning barn.

"Hang on!"

He'd seen a wooden ladder leaning up against the barn earlier, and now he pulled his shirt up to his mouth and headed to the back.

Flames shot out of the half-open door, but he spotted the ladder, now singed, in the dirt along the back.

He jerked on it, but it fought him. "C'mon!" He kicked at it, worked it free at the top, coughed, kept wrestling it.

C'mon! *Now, Jesus, now would be—*

The ladder broke free.

He sprinted around the house, coughing, eyes watering.

The jumper had climbed half out of the harness, the shoulders off, trying to work out of the thigh straps.

"Hold on!" He slammed the ladder against the barn. It just barely reached to the second story, but enough for the jumper to get his feet on the top rung. He pushed up, balanced on the pack, and pulled his thigh free. Then the other.

Turned and started down the ladder.

Crack!

The top rung broke, then the next, and the jumper hung, feet scrambling for purchase. Crew held the ladder against the barn, his head turned from the flames, nearly unable to see.

But the ladder shook, and the jumper had gotten his feet back on the rungs, now scampering down—

Another crack, this time from the roof. The building shook—

"Hurry!"

The jumper put his feet on the outside of the ladder, hands gripping the edges—and slid.

Crew backed up just before the jumper landed, stumbling back. Crew caught him, and they both went down in the dirt.

But the jumper rolled off him, scrambled to all fours. "Run!"

Through the caged visor, the goggles, and the helmet, the gaze of the jumper landed on his.

Aw—

"C'mon, Crew!" JoJo had found her feet. "It's collapsing!"

He turned, dug dirt as his feet peddled, and she grabbed his jacket.

They sprinted out of the way just as the grand wall of the barn crashed down, right where they'd been lying.

JoJo tripped, skidded into the dirt and grass, then rolled onto her back, fetal position, her hands over her helmet.

He had fallen too, taken down by her grip on him, and now rolled, crawling back.

Flames caught on the grass, but the dirt snuffed them out, and just the wall lay, burning out, smoking like a pancake on a griddle.

He glanced over at her. She still lay, curled. "Jo—it's okay. We're okay."

She lifted her head, glanced at the fire, then pushed herself up. Her hands shook as she unsnapped her helmet, pulled it off. Dropped it in the dirt. Sweat streaked her face, matted her hair as she tore off the goggles.

Stared at him, breathing hard.

"What are you—"

He leaned over, grabbed her around the neck, and kissed her. Hard, fast, more instinct than thought, and nothing like the kiss he'd left her with last time.

Not even long enough for her to respond. Just desperation, and he pulled back, met her eyes. "You okay?"

She swallowed, nodded, reached up and hooked a hand on his wrist, as if to hold on.

Then he crushed her to himself, arms around her, also shaking a little.

Behind them, the barn still flamed, although the collapse had turned it to rubble, the flames localized. So maybe he wouldn't start the entirety of Denali National Park on fire.

He finally let her go. "What happened?"

"My primary chute got snagged. By the time I pulled my backup, I was too low to navigate the wind. The fire pulled me into its vortex." She put a hand on his face. "What are you doing here?"

Oh, that.

He ran a trembling hand across his mouth. "Long story."

"Condense." She pushed herself up from the ground.

"Four days of torture, wondering if Viper might kill me. If he didn't suspect me then, he'll certainly know now."

"Why?"

"A chopper came into the compound last night. Three men got out. I think one of them might be someone important. Wore a suit. Looked a lot like a guy I knew, but I couldn't be sure."

"Who?"

"Senator Geoff Deville. He's an Alaskan state senator. Former prosecutor with the state." He spat out ashy debris onto the ground, wiped his mouth. "He and I have a personal history."

She had also coughed, spat out soot from her lungs. "He was the one who decided to make an example out of you."

He didn't know why her putting that together jolted him. Maybe because he kept trying to believe her words... *Come back to me.* But maybe... maybe she didn't see the ex-con he did.

"Yeah. But I couldn't be sure it was him. It was dark, and it's been a while. The man was with another couple guys. One looked like a rich tourist, wore a pricey leather jacket, boots. The other guy was older, gray hair, shaggy beard, gray at the temples, jeans and a jacket. Seemed to be under duress. I heard the businessman call him Doc."

"Doc."

"Yeah. And the businessman was definitely 'the big guy.' Viper called him that, along with 'sir,' and

Jer came out and gave him a handshake and a man hug, so maybe they're related."

"So clearly, returning paid off."

"More than." He motioned to the barn. "They left the compound early this morning in the chopper. I tracked them to this barn via a GPS transmitter Rio gave me. By the time I got here, they were leaving, Jer and Viper carrying a number of silver suitcases."

"How far is the compound from here?"

"Five or six miles to the east."

She had glanced at the fire, back to him. "And the fire?"

"That was me. I got inside, found a pallet of small industrial containers along with smaller canisters about the size of a fire extinguisher. I saved one and then I torched the barn."

Her eyes widened. "You burned the barn?"

"It was the only way I could think of to destroy it before they moved it."

In the distance, she heard a chopper's blades.

"We should move," she said, grabbing his arm. "They're coming in with a water dump."

"I need the ATV!"

He took off, despite her shout, for where he'd left the vehicle, jumped on, and turned it around, away from the drop zone just as the chopper pounded the air overhead.

Water gushed down over him, wetting his body as he motored out of the spray. JoJo had stepped back, away from the deluge.

He motored up, his body drenched. "Well, I'm not hot anymore."

She smiled, shook her head. "No, you're still hot." A grin.

And he would have maybe gotten off, reached for her, ready for the nightmare to be over, but he heard shouts from the forest.

Some of her smokejumper buddies emerged, full run, carrying Pulaskis, the biggest man perching a chain saw over his shoulder and a couple women also armed with shovels.

They entered the yard, breathing hard, and stared at the smoldering barn, then at soggy Crew and sooty JoJo.

The big guy with the chain saw lowered it to the ground, sighed. "Aw. All the fun is over."

"Very funny, Hammer," JoJo said.

Hammer, huh? But Crew looked at the blaze, now sizzling, and all he could think was, oh he hoped so. He really hoped so.

EIGHT

"SO, YOU AND CREW, HUH? I KNEW she had a thing for you."

JoJo looked up into the common area of the women's barracks, where Skye sat on a sofa, feet up, flicking through the channels on the flatscreen.

From outside, the evening sun cast into the room, still bright, although it had lost some of its steam. It tarried above the mountainscape to the west, a fiery ball of orange and gold.

She glanced around the room, but the other jumpers, Tori and Cadee, along with the female hotshots, Raine and Sanchez, had already gone to dinner.

Skye turned off the television, dropped the remote.

Oh, so this was a *conversation*. JoJo dropped into a nearby overstuffed chair, pulled her wet hair around, and started to braid it. "Clearly you have thoughts."

Skye folded her legs, leaned on her knees. "I just want you to know what you're getting into here. Crew is a great guy, but he comes with . . . well, baggage."

"I already know about his father and his jail time."

"Did you know that he nearly killed a man in prison?"

She stopped braiding.

"It was a fight—a brawl, really, prison-wide—but Crew was caught up in it. His father went down, and Crew lost his mind. It was in the mess hall, and he picked up a spoon, went after the guy who hurt his father, and Rio believes that if he hadn't seen it, hadn't gotten ahold of Crew then, well, things would be much different today."

"What are you saying?"

"Crew is a great guy. But he's dangerous too."

"He's had to be. Have you seen what Rio has him doing? He's living among killers—"

"It's his job."

JoJo's mouth opened.

Skye held up her hands. "I'm not saying it's easy."

"It's horrible." Aw, forget the stupid braid. She let go of her hair. "There's this Viper guy who could kill a man with his bare hands, and a guy named Jer who just might have it out for him. He was in danger every. single. minute."

"And he agreed to do it."

"Because he has no choice." She didn't know how she found her feet. "Because someone has to go in and bring these guys to justice, so of course he said yes. Because nobody else is willing to stand up against evil."

"That's not true," Skye said, her eyes sharp. "Rio went undercover in prison to fight evil."

"And didn't he nearly get killed doing it?"

She drew in a short breath.

"And I'll bet you were terrified the entire time."

"I didn't know him then."

"And if he went back now?" She stood, hands on her hips, her voice shaking.

Skye's jaw tightened. "Rio and I are married. And we're trying to start a family and—"

"And I get that. But Crew's life matters. And what if..." She looked away, her chest thick, eyes burning. She looked back, her voice low. "He'd leave behind people too."

Skye met her gaze. Then, softly, "Are you in love with Crew, JoJo?"

A beat. "No. I mean—I don't know. Maybe. But I do know what it feels like to watch a good man go out alone, face people who mean to do him—the world—harm. What it feels like to stand at his graveside, wishing that . . ."

"That it could be someone else?"

She met Skye's gaze. "No. Yes. I don't know." She shook her head. "I just know what it feels like to be the one left behind, to feel like the world has crumbled under your feet. To not find your bearings."

Skye went silent, her expression softening. "I'm sorry."

Only then did Jo realize that tears wet her face. She wiped them aside, hard. "I just can't do it again, Skye. I just can't love someone who could die. Not again."

"Who died, Jo?"

She breathed out a breath. Shook her head.

"Jo—"

"My fiancé, okay?"

A beat. "You were engaged?"

"Sort of. I was eighteen. Right out of high

school. We were going to get married after he finished basic training. Ryan was . . . too tough for his own good. Wanted to save the world." She sank back into the chair. "He joined the Marines. Was killed during a training accident."

She had to look away from Skye's expression.

"I lost my father when I was young, so yeah, I was a little needy, and maybe Ryan and I would have split up—I was already second-guessing everything—but . . . it didn't matter."

Skye went silent. Then she uncrossed her legs and leaned forward. "This isn't about Crew and his dangerous job. Or even the risks of fighting evil."

JoJo met her gaze.

"This is about you being terrified of being broken."

"Please. I jump out of planes. I'm hardly scared of getting hurt."

"Jumping out of a plane proves to yourself, over and over, that nothing can control you, not even fear. But love . . . *love* is terrifying. Love tethers you to someone else. Love can break you."

JoJo stared at her.

"I know you're scared, Jo. I get that. You're afraid of trusting someone and having them not show up, so you hold on to your heart. Hold on to control. But love is being willing to get hurt, believing that no matter what happens, *God* will never leave us. That His love is bigger than our wounds, our fears, and that in the end, He will deliver the good He promises."

For as high as the heavens are above the earth, so great is his love for those who fear him.

And she didn't know why that verse found its way in, but . . .

"How do I love someone who risks his life?"

"I guess by believing in grace and mercy and faith. And that God is enough." Skye got up. "I'm rooting for you and Crew. I just want you to go in eyes open."

Maybe too open.

"Hopefully that's over," she said, also rising. "He found the biochemical warehouse. Burned it to the ground. What more is there?"

The look Skye gave her put a fist in her stomach.

"What?"

"I think he and Rio are having that discussion right now in our cabin."

JoJo gave it one long beat, then headed for the door.

"Jo!"

"He's not going back in, Skye!" She hit the door. Turned. "Over my dead body."

Skye winced, shook her head.

JoJo ignored her, headed out to the guest cabin, where Skye and Rio stayed in a suite the few times he came around. The woman also snuck out to meet him at their home in town.

Complicated.

She could hear the conversation from the yard as she approached.

"Are you serious? I told you—Viper made me. I go back in there and I'm a dead man."

The return voice emerged smaller, tighter. Rio. "We have no choice. We have to track the suitcases. Figure out their next move."

A sound, something breaking, and she stilled right outside the door. What—

"Sorry," Crew said, and he did sound quieter. "That was an accident."

"It's just a glass. But you should calm down, Crew."

"I'm calm."

She braced her hand on the wall, just outside the stoop. Good. At least one of them was.

"We know they're highly funded. Once Jamie finds the source, we can track it. But in the meantime, we need to know their endgame, or at least what they're up to."

Silence.

"Crew. I'll clean it up. Listen. The sooner you get back, the sooner we finish this."

And just like that, the screen door slammed open. Crew stepped out, standing on the step, holding a rag to his hand, just breathing.

She flattened herself against the building, but of course, he could just look over and see her. But he seemed not to. He raised his face to the sky, closed his eyes, breathed in air.

Her heart thumped, seeing him standing, hands on his hips, legs planted, Lumberjack Batman almost steadying himself.

Then Rio. "Crew. Come back inside."

Silence as Crew just breathed.

"What are you doing?"

Crew sighed. "Just remembering what freedom smells like."

Then he turned and headed back inside.

And she just sank against the cabin, her hands on her face, trying not to weep.

No. This wasn't right. *Please, God.*

"For my thoughts are not your thoughts, neither are your ways my ways," declares the Lord. *"As the heavens are higher than the earth, so are my ways*

higher than your ways and my thoughts than your thoughts."

She leaned up, also stared at the heavens. And then Rio's words thrummed inside her. *We need to know their endgame, or at least what they're up to.*

Wait. Yes.

She stepped up on the stoop, then opened the door and went inside.

Rio looked up from where they studied a map at the kitchen table. Crew too, and something like pain washed over him.

She ignored it. "I know exactly what their next move is."

Rio frowned, but Crew drew in a breath.

"But you're going to have to trust me."

And Crew just smiled.

So, his happy reunion with Rio hadn't gone down quite like he'd hoped.

First, Rio's "What are you doing here?" had started their conversation-slash-interrogation on the dark side when he'd walked up to where Crew was helping the team unload their chopper.

Then he'd dragged Crew away to his guest suite—nice digs. Kitchen and living room combo, a small bedroom and bath. Clean. A lot nicer than his digs at the SOR compound, even the one that had been torched. Maybe he should be a smokejumper. The thought had hit him more than a few times as he'd watched the crew douse the barn, working together to clean it up, keep it from spreading into the larger wilderness.

JoJo had kept the source of the fire under her hat—or bandana, as it were—and he was just fine with letting them believe it might've been lightning.

Confession would only raise more questions, and that would lead to classified conversations and . . .

Although maybe Rio didn't care how classified the debrief, a.k.a. shouting, might be.

"Sit." He pointed to a kitchen chair.

Crew pulled out the chair, turned it around, straddled it.

Rio walked away, shaking his head, then rounded. "Seriously? You're supposed to be at the SOR compound."

Crew held up his hands. "Calm down. I found the warehouse." He cut his voice low. "And torched it."

Rio's eyes widened. "What?"

"I saved a container of the bioweapon so we

could analyze it. It's on the chopper." He even got up as if to get it.

"Stay put." Rio paced the cabin, his hand behind his neck.

Something wasn't right. "What's going on?"

He looked at Crew. "Please tell me you stuck around long enough for the big guy to show up."

"As a matter of fact, I did." He didn't mean his snappy tone, but sheesh, Rio was treating him like . . . well, like the desperate and scared eighteen-year-old kid he'd met so many years ago.

Not that guy anymore. Even if he might be sick of this gig, he wasn't going to run.

Not until he completed his mission.

Check.

"They showed up last night. Three guys. A couple fancy guys, and another they called Doc."

Rio seemed to calm down a little, leaning on the arm of his sofa. "So, three guys."

"Yeah, but the businessman was clearly the bossman. Jer knew him. Gave him a weird hug. They spent the night, then headed out to the farm early this morning."

"You followed them."

"I put a tracker on the bird—nearly got caught too—but yeah, found the warehouse."

"You destroyed it all?"

"No. They left with a number of suitcases. I destroyed the rest." He met Rio's eyes. "Mission completed."

Silence. Rio got up, walked to the window, shoved his hands into his pockets.

And Crew's chest simply tightened.

Too much silence.

"No."

"Yes," Rio said quietly. "This isn't over."

Crew's voice pitched low. "I stole an ATV. And I'm sure Viper has the barn on camera. There is no way he won't know what I did. I can't go back."

That's when Rio went to the faucet and pulled down a glass, filled it, handed it to Crew. "Just for a second. Breathe."

He didn't want to breathe. He took a drink, set the glass down on the table.

"This is bigger than we thought," Rio said quietly.

"No duh, Sherlock. I've been saying that from the beginning."

Rio's eyes narrowed. "Which is why you need to go back in, figure out what's really going on."

And that was when he lost it. Sure, fury had risen at NASCAR speed, but frankly, he'd been waging this argument in his head for the past four days, knowing—just knowing—that Rio would pull this.

He got it—of course he did. Rio was a righteous warrior. He'd done crazy—off-the-grid crazy—things in his tenure as an undercover agent. Like join a jailbreak to keep his target—and, of course, a kidnapped firefighter—alive. He'd walked into bullets more than once, according to legend.

But Crew wasn't Rio. Didn't have Rio's badge, was still just an informant.

Which in some books equaled *snitch* or *squealer*, or the prison term—*narc*.

So that was a lovely comparison. And maybe why he'd found himself on his feet, shouting. Why, a few minutes later, he'd accidentally knocked his water across the room, shattering the glass. Whoops. Why, after he'd cut himself trying to clean up the glass, he'd found himself storming outside to the stoop to just . . . breathe.

Stop himself from hitting someone—maybe Rio—to remind himself . . .

Well, he didn't know. He just lifted his face to the sunshine, breathed in the mountain air, redolent with the scent of fresh-cut grass, the pine from the nearby mountains, even the scent of dinner cooking in the mess hall.

Life. The life he wanted but couldn't, apparently, have.

Do not fear, for I am with you; do not be dismayed, for I am your God. I will strengthen you and help you; I will uphold you with my righteous right hand.

He didn't know where the words, the voice came from, but he closed his eyes and listened.

His father's voice when Crew had arrived in prison angry, scared, ready for a fight. Crew hadn't expected to see the old man—found out later that he'd requested a change of location.

He hadn't expected the changed man. The Bible-believing man.

Hadn't expected the wounds of his father's arrest and incarceration to be healed by his own sentence.

Yes. He'd been set free in prison, and maybe, if he saw this through . . .

Rio called him back inside.

He'd opened his eyes, stared at the heavens. *Show me the way, Lord.*

"What are you doing?"

He turned. "Just remembering what freedom smells like."

He'd made up his mind by the time he stepped back in, spotted Rio dumping the glass into a trash can. Then he took a map off the top of the refrigerator and spread it out on the table.

Crew stood over it. Pointed to where the warehouse was. And that's when the door banged open.

She stood there, in the frame of the door, her brown hair down and wet, her eyes big, standing in a white T-shirt and cargo pants, flip-flops, fierce, strong, light casting behind her like she might be . . . and now maybe he was getting a little loopy, but . . . an angel.

A really angry, almost belligerent angel, given the look on her face. "I know exactly what their next move is."

Crew stood up. Stared at her, drew in a breath. Oh no.

"But you're going to have to trust me." She met his eyes, almost a dare in it.

Oh, so that's where they were, huh? He smiled. Nodded.

"What?" Rio said. He turned. "You shouldn't be here."

"This is exactly where she should be," Crew said. "She was there. She saw their operation. She found the nightshade greenhouse."

Rio shook his head.

"And I know what their plan is," JoJo said. "Come with me."

She headed out the door, and Crew raised an eyebrow to Rio, then followed her.

"Let's just brief the entire crew," Rio said and followed him out.

JoJo stalked over to the administrative offices, glancing over at Crew. Grinning.

What—

Then she banged inside. "Jamie? You still here?"

Jamie came out of the room she seemed to have claimed as her office sometime in the last few weeks, looked past JoJo to Crew. "What are you doing here?"

"Right?" Rio said, on their tails.

"Show him the map, Jamie," JoJo said, and Jamie stepped back to let them into her office. Jo stopped in front of a large map pinned to the wall.

A fire map. But also—"Is that the map you gave me, Jamie?"

"Yes. Superimposed on the fire map. The orange places are—"

"Where there were fires. At least in a couple areas." He pointed to the areas in green on the map. "And this blue circle is today's warehouse."

"Yes," said JoJo. "And this orange circle"—she

pointed to a spot just north of town—"is called the Refuge. They had fire, were evacuated. But south of that, a homestead was mysteriously poisoned. Chickens killed. A woman was affected. Nearly died."

He ran a hand over his mouth. "Yes. And this is where you found your dead wolf." He touched the map north of the SOR compound, then tracked the river north. "There was a fire at this village."

"And north of there, dead salmon, according to Vince and Cadee," Jamie said.

Another orange circle.

"The plane went down in that area," said JoJo. "It caused the fire that spread to the village, but . . . it's possible that was part of the endgame."

"They wanted the plane to crash," Rio said, also studying the map. "Everywhere they've circled has been a fire."

"And maybe poison. Fire used as a cover-up," JoJo said, taking a step back, arms akimbo.

Rio was nodding, and even Crew could see him doing the math, but just in case . . . "There are two areas left."

"This one is a closed community," said Jamie. "Five homes, a large garden, a fishing pond."

"Food supply," Crew said.

"This one is the water supply that feeds into a reservoir that pipes out water to Anchorage."

Crew stilled. "First the salmon, then the wolves, and then the attempt on the Refuge."

"My guess? If they're wondering if it can affect food supply, they might target the homestead community next," JoJo said quietly.

Crew's mouth tightened, and he turned away, walked to the window, looked out at the grounds. A couple hotshots were building a fire in a pit out front. A guy threw a frisbee to a dog, who caught it in his mouth, ran back, wiggling with joy. He spotted Hammer in the workout area doing pull-ups. A couple other guys and a woman seemed to be cheering him on, counting.

Skye had pulled up an Adirondack chair beside another woman.

Listen, the sooner you get back, the sooner we finish this.

"Okay," he said, sighing, turning. "I'll do it."

Rio nodded.

JoJo shook her head. "No. That's not the way. We go warn the village and wait. Then we catch them in the act and then . . ." She looked at Rio. "Then you have what you need to take down their operation. And no one"—she walked over to Crew, slid her hand into his, turned back to Rio—"no one has to die."

What she said. But Crew just met Rio's gaze, held it.

Finally. "Okay." But Rio pointed at JoJo. "But I hope, for Crew's sake, that you're right."

NINE

I HOPE, FOR CREW'S SAKE, THAT you're right.

Rio's words played in JoJo's brain, thumping as the campfire sparked into the hazy dim-lit night. She sat on a half-hewn log facing the campfire, wrung out but wanting to linger.

Wanting to watch Crew as the firelight shimmered in his dark eyes, glinting against the gold inside, while a slight smile tweaked his face. Wanting to enjoy the way, over the last couple hours, he'd seemed to unwind.

Belong.

He threw a frisbee to Jubal, the scruffy brown labradoodle that had made his home with them from parts unknown, and maybe, in a way, they were all strays, now pack animals.

And the pack stuck together. Maybe another reason why she had stuck with the crew when they'd headed north for the summer.

Tucker was clearly their alpha male leader, although Jade certainly played alpha female. Her boyfriend, Crispin, had shown up for the night too, all tight smiles and secrets. To JoJo's knowledge, he still skirted the edges of the bigger three-letter organizations, some of whom might still believe him dead.

He might be the future look of Crew, a mysterious warrior who silently saved the world.

Oh brother. Her Batman version of Crew had clearly gone to her head.

A log fell, and she picked up a stick, moved it back into the center of the fire ring.

Are you in love with Crew?

Oh. She feared the answer. It felt too quick, too much like she might be losing a piece of herself. And yes, every time he looked at her, something shifted inside her.

Aw, it had to be joy.

Crew leaned back, and for some reason looked over at her, something in his eyes, and for a moment, she stood in the office, him holding her hand as if they stood together.

Two, better than one.

I know you're scared, Jo. I get that. Love is being willing to get hurt, believing that no matter what happens, God will never leave us.

A couple of the hotshots were talking about climbs they wanted to take on their off days. And Vince and Cadee had gotten up, walked away from the crew, holding hands.

She spotted Crispin, his hand woven with Jade's. They'd gone from zero to dating so fast that people hadn't even realized Crispin was back from the dead before he'd announced he was following Jade back to Alaska.

Maybe it didn't matter how quickly she fell for Crew. Maybe it only mattered how much of her heart she'd give him.

He's dangerous.

Yeah, Skye had hit it on the head. She had no idea how dangerous.

"It's late. You guys okay with me bunking with you?" Crew said, pushing himself up from the chair.

"Grab a bunk. There's a couple extra sleeping bags hanging in the entry," said Logan.

Crew walked past her, glanced down at her,

and how terribly obvious would it be if she got up and followed?

He stopped. "Walk a guy home?"

A couple smiles, from Jade, then Crispin.

She took his hand, let him lead her from the firepit toward the cabins. He wove his fingers through hers, walked in quiet.

"I know you want to chase wolves," he said, his voice easy, low, "but you have a good thing going here with this team, Jo. Maybe you stick this out for a while."

She looked up at him.

"Maybe I become a smokejumper." He lifted a shoulder.

"You'd make an amazing smokejumper," she said, but weirdly, the idea had her seizing up inside. What—

And maybe he saw it, because he frowned, then pulled her away, between the cabins, into the shadows. "What's wrong?"

She shook her head. "Nothing. I'm being stupid."

He leaned back against the cabin, pulled her into his embrace. "You're not stupid. You figured out that map. That was brilliant."

She ran her hands over his chest, smoothing out his shirt. He'd showered, smelled like cedar and pine and his own perfect musk. "I need to tell you something." She'd been avoiding thinking of it ever since she'd confessed to Skye. But, okay, here went nothing. "I was engaged."

He stiffened, stood up, set her away from him. "What?"

"Many years ago. To my high-school sweetheart." She stepped back from him, met his eyes. "He was killed."

His mouth opened. "Oh, wow, I'm so sorry."

She nodded, her throat weirdly thick. "He joined the Marines, died in training. It was a freak drowning accident but ... anyway, it's crazy, because I'm fine with any of those guys jumping out of planes, risking their lives, but you ..." She shook her head. "Sorry. I've been haunted for the past four days by the thought of you back in that camp, and now, I don't know ... I just don't want anything to happen to you."

He stepped up to her, lifted her face, his hand under her chin. "I think that's the nicest thing anyone has ever said to me."

It was?

But she didn't have time to respond, because he kissed her. Sweetly, his lips against hers, and then deeper as his arms moved around her. He backed against the cabin again, pulled her into him, and his kiss turned from gentle to possessive, to belonging and oneness, to beauty and peace.

A kiss that explored and discovered and knew, and she found herself with her arms around him, discovering and knowing too.

Yes, she was falling for this man. And maybe life was dangerous, but maybe it was supposed to be met by dangerous men who stood for and believed in something.

All the way to the end.

And it struck her, even as Crew leaned away, met her eyes, that maybe Crew needed her to have the courage to love a man like him.

No matter what it cost her.

God has not given us a spirit of fear, but of power and of love and of a sound mind.

Okay then. Eyes open.

He blew out a breath, met her eyes, his chest rising and falling, studying her. Then, "I think I need to leave now."

Oh.

He leaned in, kissed her again, the lightest touch on her lips, then stood, let out a breath, and pushed her away. "You're right. I just can't stop kissing you." Then he turned and said, "See you in the morning, Wolf Girl." And winked.

And she had nothing left of her heart.

She felt partially restored when she met him the next morning at the coffee pot in the mess hall, but he'd changed into fresh jeans and a clean blue thermal shirt, maybe Rio's doing, that perfectly highlighted his dark eyes, and he nudged her hip as he came up to her. So there went that.

He turned to her as she poured coffee. "Rio talked Dodge Kingston into giving us a ride to the homesteads."

"Dodge Kingston?"

"He's a chopper pilot in the area, runs a search and rescue branch up here. Rio didn't want to utilize the smokejumpers, so we're going in, just him and me—"

She rounded on him. "And me."

He gave her a grim look.

"I am going with you. It was my idea. And if the SOR shows up, you'll need help."

"What are you going to do? You're not trained in law enforcement."

"Neither are you!"

He winced, and—"Oh, Crew, I didn't mean—"

"You're right." He sipped his black coffee. "I'm not. But I do have a little experience with these guys."

"And I have experience getting people to evacuate. Which is exactly what we'll need to do if they've doused their fields and plan to set them on fire. I'll know how to slow it down, and I can call in our crew."

"Your crew is going with you." This from Hammer, who'd joined them. "Jamie filled in Logan, who filled in me and the guys, and you're wrong if you think you're going to save this village by yourselves. Hogging all the heroism." He shook his head but flashed a smile before he took a sip of his coffee.

A smile? She nearly choked on hers.

Hammer glanced at Crew. "Wheels up in ten minutes." He walked away.

Crew turned back to her. "Does that guy have the hots for you?"

She lifted a shoulder. "Does it matter?"

Crew grinned. "Nope." He looked like he might kiss her, so she pushed past him.

"To the chopper, Batman."

Ten minutes later, she climbed into the big Bell 429 parked on the tarmac. She met the pilot—Dodge was a good-looking guy with dark hair and aviator sunglasses and a grim set to his mouth as he talked with Rio.

She had geared up, carried her helmet and gloves, a jacket, and now sat next to Logan in the chopper. Crew and Hammer climbed in behind them. Rio sat in front. She noticed a gear box too, so the guys had at least brought tools. And they all wore their canvas pants and yellow Nomex shirts, held helmets and jackets as well.

Hopefully this wouldn't turn into a firefight.

They donned headphones and lifted off, and she felt a little like they might be going into combat, the way the chopper arched, headed west. Maybe Dodge had been a military pilot.

She stared out the window, spotted the Copper River meandering below them and then the tributaries cutting away through the woods.

They couldn't poison a river, not with the fast-running currents. But a reservoir?

And a small food supply?

"We're coming up on the Birch Creek community."

She looked out to see a large cleared area bordered by a dozen or so greenhouses. Across a dirt road, a fenced area held clusters of beef cattle.

And nestled among the trees, five small homes with vehicles parked in dirt driveways. A thin dirt road led through the forest toward a gravel road in the distance.

Remote. Contained. The perfect test site for a bioweapon.

She sat back, met Crew's hard-jawed gaze.

What? They had a veritable army with them. What did he think was going to happen?

"Crew," Rio said through the comms. "Does the SOR have a drone?"

Crew frowned. "Yeah. They use it for surveillance. Why?"

JoJo leaned over and looked again out the window. Oh, that was why. What looked like a prehistoric mosquito in the sky, nine feet across, ten feet tall, a tank on the bottom—it was a monster—sweeping over the garden with its four arms, spraying its payload.

It then swooped away toward the beef pasture.

No, oh no—

"Because," said Rio, "I think they're already here."

"Put us on the ground, Dodge!" Rio's voice, but Crew's inner shout as he watched the drone circle the field.

He couldn't tell if it had deployed the poison or not. *Please, God, not*—

"Just open the hatch and hand me a gun," Hammer said, unclipping from his harness.

Crew looked at him, wide-eyed, as Hammer wrenched open the chopper door. What? He was in a Francis Ford Coppola movie, flying over Vietnam.

"Get back inside!" Rio shouted.

Hammer had found a gun strapped to the back of the pilot's chair—a .44 Magnum. Crew glanced at JoJo. She held up her hands, shook her head, so not hers—probably belonged to Dodge.

Hammer leaned out the door, aimed, and popped off five shots. At least one hit the drone, and it flipped, spun, and crashed, shattering in the middle of the cow pasture.

He shut the door. "Now set us down."

Crew watched as he sat down. Okay then.

Still, the second they set down, Rio unstrapped, then jumped out of the chopper, running, head down, toward the downed drone.

Get a mask. He didn't know why he thought that, but—okay, probably a mask wouldn't help. But the whole *bioweapon* term had his skin crawling.

He also unharnessed and opened the door, got out, the blades above slowing their spin. They sat in the middle of the field, dust in the air. They were probably breathing toxins right now.

JoJo probably thought the same thing, because she had donned her handkerchief over her nose. Another brilliant move.

She made a better undercover agent than he did. Sheesh.

Not that he cared, because the sense of tomorrow, a.k.a. hope, still sat under his skin. Last night, hanging out with her crew, the easy belonging—it'd felt like his father's stories of his buddies in the Marines. The kind of guys you could count on, who had your back.

And maybe it was a foolish dream, but yes. He could fly with her, fight fires with her . . .

Be like Skye and Rio.

He could still taste JoJo's kiss, still feel her in his arms.

Focus. Rio ran back to him. "I found the canister. It's empty. Not sure if it emptied in the crash or—"

"How big is it?"

"About the size of a fire extinguisher."

"So, nine liters? Yeah, that's about the size of one of the canisters," Crew said.

"These things only have about a mile range," said Hammer. "So the drone driver has to be around here somewhere."

"And he'd want to make sure he delivered the payload," said JoJo. She stood behind them, a little stricken.

"Okay, listen, smokejumpers, get into the homes, tell the people to stay inside."

"We should burn the field," said Logan. "Keep it from spreading."

"We need to talk to them, tell them what's happening," Vince said. "We can't just burn their food supply."

"Yes—go. Talk to them." Rio looked at Crew. "You, me, and"—he pointed to Hammer—"you. Get back in the chopper. Let's see if we can find them."

He handed Crew a weapon from his shoulder holster. "Do not shoot unless you are shot at."

"I remember my training."

Rio nodded, then took off for the chopper, Crew behind him. He and Hammer climbed into the back.

Hammer hooked in but sat on the edge, again in some war movie.

Crew sat at the other edge of his seat, belted in, but opened the door.

Dodge took off.

As they rose, Crew spotted the team running toward the houses.

And it just hit him—the spread of evil. It landed on the living, infected them without knowing, and it felt so unfair.

So brutally wrong.

So maybe, just like he'd said to JoJo, he was the good guy. Should start believing that.

Dodge soared over the forest—thick, dense, and unforgiving. He hadn't a hope of finding Viper or Jer or any of the other SOR members.

Maybe they'd already escaped.

Dodge angled them down the road, maybe thinking the same thing. No grimy truck or even mud-splattered ATV appeared, escaping the scene of the crime.

The firefighters had emerged, and Crew watched from afar and a thousand feet up as they lit a fire at the edge of a vegetable crop. He couldn't make them out from here, but it seemed that they positioned themselves along the edge of the fire, using their shovels to keep it from escaping.

A man and woman had come out into the field, riding four-wheelers, driving the cattle toward a barn nearer the cluster of homes.

They'd have to burn that field too.

He hung on, a little sick.

The smoke rose, cluttered the sky, picked up by the wind and spread out over the property. Dodge angled around the fire and headed north to where the road disappeared into the woods.

He finally turned around at a ranch where a woman and a boy, maybe age ten, came out of the house, cupping their hands over their eyes.

He hoped Hammer didn't wave with his gun hand.

They headed south again, where the fire burned now at the far end of the garden. A couple of the smokejumpers had started to dig a line around the field the drone had doused. Not a huge area, so maybe it wouldn't have to be completely destroyed.

Then again, even a little poison could bleed into the soil, turn it lethal.

Dodge set them down south of the fire, the winds blowing it north, and they piled out. Vince and Logan jogged over from where they were cutting a line in the field. "Anything?"

"No. They're in the wind," Rio said, and glanced at Crew.

And it hit him like a sledge.

They'd failed. They hadn't connected the drone with the SOR, which meant . . .

He gave a tight nod. Then he stuck the gun in his belt, headed toward the fire. Logan tended it at the far end of the garden, the smoke dying now, turning to gray, a little white. The crops lay in ash, the tomato vines curled, the cabbages in sooty balls. They hadn't all burned, but they'd be tilled under and maybe reburned.

Or who knew how corrupted the soil might be, even tilled and burned and left to rest?

Maybe it would never turn healthy and pure.

They needed someone who could test the soil to come out here and ensure it was safe. Then again, maybe a reporter was a better idea.

Get the word out to the public.

Warn people.

"Hey. Where's JoJo?" Crew asked.

Logan looked around, a handkerchief over his nose and mouth, his goggles sooty. "She went to talk with the homesteaders, give them an update." He gestured over to the barn where a number of people congregated. Crew headed over to them.

Two women, one with a baby on her hip, a handkerchief holding back her hair. She wore jeans and a sweatshirt. Another woman, the arms of her flannel shirt folded up, graying hair held back in a ponytail. It occurred to him that this might be multiple generations of the same family.

Two men, one older, graying, still sturdy. The other in his mid-thirties, wearing a blue stained gimme cap and Carhartt overalls.

"Hey," Crew said. "You guys okay?"

The younger man rounded on him. "What do you think? That's our entire crop."

"Not the entire crop. We have early berries and baby potatoes." This from the blonde.

He looked at her, sighed, shook his head. "Who did this?"

"A local revolutionary group. We think they used your farm to test a bioweapon."

Silence, and maybe he shouldn't have said that.

The woman turned away, her hand over her mouth.

The younger man stared at him, clearly unable to speak.

"How dangerous is it?" the older man asked. "Are our cattle affected?"

"I don't know. Give them a good wash. Keep them out of the field. Do you have grain?"

"Yes. But it's our emergency supply."

"Gordon. It's okay. We'll do what can. God won't let us go hungry." He'd put his hand on the younger man's arm.

Gordon glanced at him, shook his head again, walking away.

"My son is just angry."

"I'm angry, sir. This is wrong. And I'm sorry we didn't get here sooner."

The man stuck his hand out. "Mike."

Crew met it. "Uh, Crew. Sterling."

"Thanks, Crew, for trying to help. I suppose we could have waited until the authorities came out to test the soil, but the woman said that it could get into the soil, so we decided to burn."

"Sorry about that. We'll get authorities out here to test your soil as soon as we can. Until then, don't let the cattle graze, and boil your water. Um ..." He looked around. "Have you seen her—the woman? Her name is Jo."

Mike frowned, looked past him, then to the house. "No. I do remember her talking to someone." He turned back. "I don't see him either."

Crew stilled. "Can you describe him?"

"Sure. Big guy. He came up just when we brought in the cattle. Asked if we needed help. The woman—Jo?—was talking to Gordon. I went into the house to get Patty, and when I came out ... yeah, I don't remember seeing them."

"Big guy," Crew said, his throat closing. "Short dark-blond hair. Beard. Did you happen to see a snake tattoo on his neck?"

"Yeah, that's him. Said he was driving by and saw the smoke."

Crew couldn't breathe. Couldn't swallow. Couldn't move.

"You okay, son?"

Maybe he nodded, he didn't know. And somehow, he managed to turn around, to start running, to sort out his brains and find his voice by the time he reached Rio.

"What?" Rio said, rounding. "Crew, what's going on—oh no."

"Yes." He grabbed his knees, breathing hard. "The SOR's got her." He stood up, looked at Crew. "Jeremiah took Jo."

Then he walked over to the edge of the chopper, hung onto the tail, and lost it, right there on the poisoned earth.

TEN

SHE SIMPLY HADN'T SEEN IT COMING.
One minute she'd been talking to Gordon about the fire and what to do with the soil.

The next, a man had walked into the barn, his dark-blond hair cut short. He wore a beard, a friendly, hands-in-pocket posture, and smiled at the older man. "You got some trouble I can help with?"

He'd looked familiar, but she couldn't place him, not in the shadows of the barn.

She'd thought maybe Gordon knew him. He'd shaken his hand and told him the fire crew had everything under control. Then the man turned to her, and said, "I know a couple firefighters."

Which had her asking who he might know while Gordon walked away.

And the minute Gordon had left the barn, *bam!*

He'd slugged her. An explosion that had sent her careening, dazed, and she barely knew herself as he grabbed her arm, brought her to her feet.

And moments later, threw her into the back seat of his truck.

She lay in the well behind the seat, trying to clear her head. Her face felt shattered, the pain knocking against her brains, but she pushed up, grabbed the back of the seat.

Turned.

The farm sat a half mile away, getting smaller, the smoke rising to obscure it.

She reached for the door handle, but it didn't move.

"Child locks," said the man, and she looked at him and it clicked.

Snake tattoo. She'd seen the man at the compound. "You're with the SOR."

He turned onto the road parallel to the farm, then skidded to a stop.

What—

He turned to her then.

She tried to dodge him, but he hit her again,

this time on her ear, and her head rang. Still, she put up her hands, screaming, as he scrambled over the seat.

He grabbed her neck, pressed her into the seat, and then held her down as he grabbed her hands, zip-tying them behind her back.

Then he tied her legs while she fought to kick him, tears hot on her face as she kept screaming.

He slapped her, but she hardly felt it with the cascade of other pain—and then, somehow, he'd gotten a roll of duct tape. He plastered it against her mouth.

"Shut. Up."

And he pushed her again into the well behind the seats and got out.

In a moment, the truck started up again.

God, please!

She tried to listen for changes in roadway, guessed they'd landed on pavement, but after an hour, her brain hadn't a clue where they might be going.

Her face had stopped hurting. And all she could think was . . .

Crew would find her.

And probably get killed trying to save her.

She closed her eyes. Heard the verse thrumming inside her. *God has not given us a spirit of fear, but of power and of love and of a sound mind.*

Yeah, maybe. But right now, fear seemed to be winning, and yes, clouding her mind, running over her with the what-ifs.

She wasn't stupid. They'd taken her because they wanted Crew.

Tire crunched against dirt, and the truck slowed. Shouting, a gate squealed, and her gut tightened.

Then the truck stopped, the door opened, and hands pulled her out. She stood, her legs wanting to give out on her as she was taken into the compound. A few men moved around, some with weapons, others hauling wood, a couple with dogs, all of them eyeing her.

The man crouched and pulled out a knife. She stiffened, but he broke her leg ties, stood back up.

And then she spotted him, coming out of the main building, wearing a black canvas shirt, a pair of jeans, boots, and a smirk. Scar under his eye, brown hair, beard . . .

Viper.

He walked over and held out his hand to her captor. "Good job, Jer. Any trouble grabbing her?"

"She got a little mouthy."

Viper glanced at her, nodded, then walked over, and just like that, ripped the tape from her mouth. She'd already moistened free the area around her lips, but still, the shock made her cry out.

"Go ahead. Scream. No one will hear you."

She wanted to shout at him, and of course, say something stupid like "Wait until Crew gets here."

Except, that might be the very last thing Crew should do. Because Crew returning to save her might be akin to suicide.

Maybe Viper read her mind, because he gave her a smile and said, "We'll see if he comes for you." Then he grabbed her by the arm and marched her to the guest cabin. Opened the door and pushed her inside.

She stumbled, fell to her knees, but managed not to fall face-first and scrub her chin on the floor.

When she rolled over, sitting, Viper stood in the frame. "Don't get brave."

Then he turned and slammed the door. The lock bolted from the outside.

Yeah, she didn't have a lot of brave left, thank you.

Except a voice thrummed inside her.

The Lord is a refuge for the oppressed, a strong-hold in times of trouble. Those who know your name trust in you, for you, Lord, have never forsaken those who seek you.

Oh, she hoped so. She pushed herself back to the wall, closed her eyes. *Help me, Lord.*

The prayer felt feeble, however, as though it bounced back from the ceiling.

Still, she sent it up again.

Her heartbeat began to slow, her mind clearing. Barking lifted from outside, along with voices in the compound. A bell—dinner.

Her stomach gave a traitorous growl.

But with the men inside, she had to get free.

She stretched her hands against the ties, found some give, even if she couldn't ease them free. Still, it was enough for her to move her body into the gap and bring her arms to the front.

Then she bit the end of the tie and pulled the loop as tight as she could.

Please, let this work.

She lifted her arms up, took a breath, then pulled her hands down, wrenching her wrists apart.

The tie snapped.

She looked at it a moment, her breath caught.

Seriously? Okay then.

She found her feet, headed toward the door, tried it.

Nothing.

Except—footsteps landed on the porch.

She stilled, then backed up, hit the wall and slid down, grabbing the broken tie and putting her hands behind her back.

The lock slid back, and the door opened.

Not snake tattoo man. Not Viper. An older man stepped inside. Wait—Crew's words stirred in her mind. *Older. Gray hair, scraggly beard . . .*

Doc.

He stepped in, closed the door behind him.

Seemed to be under duress.

Yep. Because the man raised a hand. "I won't hurt you."

She leaned back, her knees up to kick just in case he came close. Her gaze flashed past him, on the door. Maybe she could overpower—

"I'm looking for Maria."

She raised an eyebrow. "Um . . . I don't—"

"She's with the fire crew. You're one of them, right?"

She nodded.

"I thought maybe . . ." He sighed. "You're not her."

"No."

"Maria Cortez."

"We . . . I don't know her."

He sighed then, nodded. "Okay."

Then he turned to leave.

"Wait, um . . ."

He turned. "I can't help you. I can't help any-one."

Then he walked out the door. She heard the lock click, like a hammer in her soul.

No. The only one who could help her . . . was her.

There was no way out but in. But suddenly his boss had turned on him.

"Rio, listen to me. C'mon."

"I just need a full minute to think here, Crew." Of course they had to wage the argument through the headsets of the chopper as Dodge flew them back to Copper Mountain. At least he'd gotten Rio to agree to land in town.

Rio wanted to alert the sheriff.

"With what proof?" Crew had practically shouted, right there in the field, after he'd wiped his mouth—and hadn't that been fun? Losing it in front of the SJs, and even Hammer, who'd stared at him with a sort of arms-folded, tight-lipped disgust.

Or maybe that was directed at Rio, who hadn't made any friends with his "Everybody calm down" statements.

Now Crew sat shoulder to shoulder with the team, meeting their eyes, all of them grim-faced, and sure, they weren't law enforcement or even superheroes, but it seemed they'd face demons for JoJo.

Maybe for each other.

Yeah, someday . . .

Dodge called in to air control at the Copper Mountain FBO and took the chopper down.

Crew unhooked his harness, piled out, and rounded on Rio. "Full minute is up. Keys." He held out his hand. "I know you have a pickup around here I can use."

"We can use the one at the sheriff's office," Rio said.

Perfect. Wonderful. Awesome. Crew shook his head and pressed a hand to his gut. Because every image that exploded through his mind made him want to retch all over again.

Please, God. He couldn't get out anything more than that.

Maybe it was enough.

He strode across the tarmac as Hammer and Vince caught up to him. "We're going with you."

He rounded. "And get killed? Because you do know these guys aren't jerking around. They are murderers and thieves, most of them criminals, well-funded, and off their heads. And you guys fight fire."

They were unmoving, expressions dark.

"Right?"

"Yeah, not so much," Vince said. "Let's call it a second job."

Oh.

On the tarmac, the chopper fired up.

"The other SJs are heading back to base," Hammer said. "They'll fill in the team."

So, that would be an interesting conversation.

"Wouldn't be the first time this summer we've tangled with these guys," Vince said.

The chopper lifted off, dust scattering.

"Yeah, I know. Because last time, your *plane was shot down*."

"Sheesh. Thanks for that," Hammer said. "Talk about salt."

"Right?" Vince said. "My mentor at the DEA betrayed me, and he's part of all this somehow." He headed for the administrative building, where

Rio was already inside, hopefully calling the sheriff's office.

Yes. Because a truck pulled up as Crew walked in from the tarmac. A woman opened the door, hopped out. "Hey, Shasta," Rio said.

"Rio. Guys, get in the back."

They piled in, Rio in the passenger seat, and she drove them the short distance to town. Crew jumped out, strode up to Rio. "Keys."

Rio pocketed them. "Not yet."

He opened his mouth, closed it. Stared at him. "You want her to get beaten. Raped. Tortured—"

"That's enough, Crew."

"You don't know these guys like I do."

"I know exactly who these guys are! I lived with them in prison. And where do you think I got my undercover experience? This is *not* my first carnival." He blew out a breath, his eyes hot. "Yes, we will go in and get her. I swear to you, we will. But we do this wrong, we have to start all over again. They'll vanish into the woods, and if we really screw up, they'll take her with them."

Ice blew into his soul.

"So, step. back. Let's go talk to Deke, and let me get authorization."

Authorization. He fisted his hands, shook them in front of him, then exhaled hard and followed Rio inside, Vince and Hammer behind him.

Deke stepped out of his office. "Rio, what's going on?"

"SOR attacked a small farm outside town. Doused them. We had to burn the crops. We'll need to get ahold of the Anchorage office and get some folks up there to test the soil and the cattle. But we have a bigger problem."

Another man had come out of the conference room, holding a cup of coffee. A bigger man, maybe in his fifties, brawny, although it could be partly from the nearby bakery.

"What's going on?"

"Deputy Mills," said Rio and shook his hand. He turned back to Deke. "One of our smoke-jumpers was snatched from a fire site. We think the SOR took her."

"Think? We know Viper has her." Crew slammed his hand onto the counter separating the entry and the back.

"Calm down there, son," Mills said.

Crew looked at him. "Calm. down? Do you have any idea who these guys are? The Sons of Revolution, as in Anarchy, Please. They want to dismantle society, rules, and frankly, they should scare you to your bones."

Mills looked him up and down. "Wait." He looked at Rio, back to Crew. "I've seen you in town. You're one of them. Am I supposed to be scared of you?"

"Mills. He's with us."

"Really. Because he looks exactly like the criminal element down at the Copper Mountain prison—wait. Yes. I remember you. Tough kid. Your dad transferred to the prison to babysit you."

Crew's mouth opened. "He didn't—" But yes, that's exactly what his father had done. And had died for it, the smaller facility lacking the resources to treat his cancer.

Breathe. *A gentle answer turns away wrath, but a harsh word stirs up anger.*

His father's words, rising inside him.

Right. "Yes. My father was there. Good man—"

"Who killed someone."

Crew clamped his mouth shut. Took a deep breath.

Turned.

And maybe it was sharper than he meant, and he did raise his fists again, in frustration—

But he didn't mean to bump Mills's coffee hand.

Hot liquid splashed over the deputy's arm, his shirt, and Mills backed up, shouted.

Rio had his back to them, glanced over his shoulder, but too late—

"Is that a gun?" Mills growled.

Aw. The .44 Magnum. In his belt.

And just like that, Mills overpowered the donuts, grabbed Crew by the neck, and shoved him against the wall.

He winced, but mostly from the shock, and then Mills kicked out his legs. "Stay still."

And he knew the drill. Because suddenly he was prisoner number AK-38905-X, mouth shut, face to the wall, being searched.

"Mills! Back off." Rio.

"He's working with the FBI," said the sheriff.

"He's a felon with a gun. That's statute 18 USC 922(g)(1), which makes it unlawful for anyone who has been convicted of a felony to be in possession of a firearm." He grabbed Crew's wrist, pulled it behind him, snapped on a cuff.

Then the other. Bracelets.

"The sentence can be up to ten years in prison. Maybe it's time you join your old man back inside, huh?"

He spun him around.

"I can't," Crew said quietly. "He's dead."

A beat, and Mills jaw tightened. "Let's go."

"Mills—" the sheriff said, and Deputy Mills

stopped, his grip tight on Crew's arm. "He just spilled your coffee."

Silence. "What kind of outfit are you running here, Sheriff, that you're going to let a felon come in here with a gun and walk back out?"

Deke sighed, looked at Crew. "Okay. Just cool off, Crew. We'll figure this out."

His mouth opened, closed, and he pinned a look on Rio.

His mentor held up a hand, his mouth a tight grimace. Shook his head.

Crew bit back the urge to jerk out of Mills's grip. He couldn't look at Vince or Hammer as Mills took him down the hall to the temporary cells in back.

Mills unlocked the door, then led Crew to a cell, opened the door.

Crew stepped inside.

"Back up against the bars."

Crew closed his eyes, stepped back so Mills could uncuff him. Good thing the deputy had restrained him for that thirty-foot walk back to lockup.

He bit that back too.

Because actually, that might not have been a bad decision. No way was Crew willingly headed back to jail, and it might have gotten ugly.

He sank onto a metal cot and stared up at the tiny window that shed light into the cell.

And plotted his escape.

ELEVEN

C'MON, JO. THINK.

She sat against the wall, the shadows long in the room. She guessed the hour late, maybe after ten. Her stomach growled.

Her jaw ached. Viper had probably left a mark.

Outside, a couple ATVs motored into the compound.

She had to get out of here. But without the cover of darkness . . .

She closed her eyes. Heard again the verse that kept replaying in her head. *For God has not given us a spirit of fear, but of power and of love and of a sound mind.*

Her mother, in her head again.

Jo, even though life feels out of control, it's not, and we're going to hold on to truth.

Yes. The words poured through her, found her bones, and stirred up Skye's words. *No matter what happens, God will never leave us . . . In the end, He will deliver the good He promises.*

And in her mind, she saw Crew sitting on the floor, on his sleeping bag, unwilling to leave her alone in a dangerous place. Heard their conversation.

They mess with you, they mess with me.

She ran her hand against her face. Yeah, well, he wasn't here. And couldn't be here.

She was on her own.

Where can I go from your spirit? Where can I flee from your presence? If I say, "Surely the darkness will hide me and the light become night around me . . ."

The verse stirred inside her. Darkness.

Hiding.

Hiding.

She stood up, walked over to where Crew had set his sleeping bag. Wooden planks. They'd squeaked and rattled.

Which meant they might be able to be moved.

Different length boards, some of them four

feet, some two, others six. One of the four-foot lengths creaked.

She stomped on it, and the opposite end moved, maybe two inches. It could be pried up. Except, with what? She no longer had her Pulaski.

But the cot had metal connecting pieces. She examined it. A metal bracket held two sections together.

She brought her foot down on the joint. The cot cracked, and another kick broke the wood from the metal. A little wrangling, and the metal piece tore off—about four inches tall, thin screws protruding from it.

Dispatching the screws, she returned to the board. Worked the metal into the crack at the loose end and started to work the board. The wood squealed on the nails, an angry old man. But it budged.

And then she worked the bracket underneath and pried it up. It broke from the other nails, and she heaved it up, again and again.

It detached from the joist.

And below it, darkness. A hiding place.

At least enough to keep them thinking she'd escaped.

She pried up the next board, a two-footer,

and worked herself into the space, onto the bare ground.

The cabin sat on four cinder blocks, weeds growing up around the foundation, the earth under the cabin cool and dark. Some debris had worked its way under over the years: brittle sticks, withered pine cones, and garbage, some fabric, wadded paper. Broken glass.

If she waited long enough, maybe the compound would fall into enough shadow for her to get away.

This could work.

She climbed back out and grimaced at the cot. Nothing she could do about that, but she moved the table and chairs over the loose boards, then climbed back into the hole, dragging the bigger board over the space, then the smaller.

She crawled away from the opening, to the edge of the foundation, and hunkered down behind the weeds, parting them enough to see the yard, or at least a portion of it.

Dogs, in cages—she'd heard them barking earlier—now ate food delivered by a couple men. The ATVs and other cars sat parked in the garage, and a few armed men roamed the camp. Beside her cabin was a larger Quonset building to one side and, from her memory, a wooden building to the other. Maybe storage.

You are my portion, Lord; I have promised to obey your words.

The only power fear had over her was to keep her from trusting God. From believing in truth. From knowing that God still held her.

Tell me what to do, Lord.

And for some reason, Psalm 37 rose in her head. *The wicked will perish: Though the Lord's enemies are like the flowers of the field, they will be consumed, they will go up in smoke.*

Smoke.

That's what she needed. A diversion.

From across the yard, movement, and she spotted the man Crew called Jer emerge from the mess hall.

A big man. Sloppy, bearded, wearing a baseball cap and a flannel shirt, jeans and boots. Carried a bowie on his belt.

He stepped out into the yard, glanced at the security, raised a hand to someone, and then headed out across the yard.

Toward the guest cabin.

What—

Oh, okay, breathe—

He reached the cabin, and a lock rattled on the door. So, Viper had padlocked her in.

Then, footsteps.

Porcelain shattered against the wall—the plate from the meal Viper had brought her earlier.

Then the door banged against the wall and footsteps pounded out.

Maybe, right now, they'd think she'd escaped. Would search the compound.

Which bought her some time.

She scrambled across the space and up into the cabin.

The plate had broken into a number of pieces, bacon grease slathered over the top. A fuel.

She grabbed the cot, ripped the fabric from the frame, and shoved it out the window.

Then she grabbed the plate pieces and slipped back under the cabin, toward the back, and parted the weeds. Nothing back here but more weeds, and farther, the tall, barbed-wire fence.

She gathered up debris—the pine cones, the paper, even the fabric, which turned out to be an oily canvas work shirt—and pushed it out of the weedy border. She rooted around until she found a piece of glass the size of her hand, probably from the old window, and then she climbed out of the cabin, crouching.

The sun still hung high enough to pour down into the yard, simmering.

She crouched in the light, building a nest of kindling—the pine cone, the twigs—and scraped the bacon grease onto the paper.

Then she found the light and angled the glass to catch it, to focus it on the bacon-greased paper.

C'mon.

Shouting from across the compound. *Don't look.*

C'mon.

Smoke lifted from the tiny mound, and she leaned down, blew on it. Kept the light focused.

Flame, so small it nearly flickered out, but she fed in more paper, and it grew. It popped to life, growing, grabbing the pine cone, and bam, she had fire.

She held the shirt to the flame, and it caught.

Grabbing it up, she peeked around the side. There, on the ground, the cot fabric.

She tossed the flaming shirt onto the fabric.

It caught, the fire devouring the fuel, and smoke rose, dark and oily. It might even catch the cabin on fire if she were lucky.

No, not lucky. Protected.

And as if God might be confirming, suddenly

the blaze caught on an old greasy tire hidden in the grass. It flamed up, consuming the grease.

The area clogged with black smoke.

More shouts, and she didn't stick around. She ducked down, let the smoke obscure her, and took off running toward the fence.

Barking.

The fence rose, taller than she'd realized. No way would she get over that, not with the barbed wire along the top.

The storage shed. It sat on cinder blocks, just like the cabin. An old log cabin but sturdy. And attached to the back, a bin, maybe for firewood. And with the window above, possibly a second floor.

She ran, leaped on it, and then pulled herself up, into the window.

Yes, a loft. And it overlooked the body of the cabin.

A storage unit, for sure. And it held a massive four-armed drone, four times the size of the field drone.

A plastic barrel sat next to it.

Probably filled with enough poison to dose the entire Eklutna Lake. The water supply of Anchorage.

The next test?

More barking. She peeked out the window and spotted the dogs loosed in the yard.

If they caught her in here, she'd be trapped.

Now what, Lord?

For in the day of trouble he will keep me safe in his dwelling; he will hide me in the shelter of his sacred tent and set me high upon a rock.

Or a house?

She headed back to the window, peeked out the back. The cabin next door had caught fire, the smoke now roiling into the sky, crackling, sparking.

Obscuring her movements.

She climbed out, then stood on the window ledge and reached for the roof.

Blamed Jade and her insistence that they keep training all the summer, because she grabbed the edge and pulled herself up to the grassy, moldy, rotting surface.

Then she lay on top, watching the chaos like a panther, and prayed.

Sorry, Dad.

Crew didn't know why that, of all thoughts, pulsed in his head as he lay on the stainless-steel bench in the jail cell.

So many stupid mistakes cluttered his brain, strangled him. And now JoJo would pay the price.

He threw an arm over his eyes, but in the darkness, it only brought to mind the image of Viper—or worse, Jer—

Okay. Not going there. He sat up, wove his fingers together behind his neck, hung his head. Breathed.

Even though life feels out of control, it's not, and we're going to hold on to truth.

JoJo's words to him in the cabin. Maybe that's why he kept thinking of his father. She'd spoken his father's verse. *Where can I go from your spirit? Where can I flee from your presence?*

He could almost see the old man walking up to him in the yard right after he'd been incarcerated. The fact he'd transferred to the prison to be near him . . . Crew didn't know what wheels his dad had greased for that to happen, but Crew had become a child in that moment, fighting not to betray the heat that wanted to wash over him.

What Mills had said was true. His father had transferred to watch over him.

To witness to him. To bring him to faith, probably, because he'd been there too when Crew had knelt before the prison altar and asked Jesus to save him.

Save him.

He closed his eyes, that moment upon him, his father's hand warm on his shoulder as he knelt next to Crew. His father's prayer after Crew had prayed his own. "Thank you, God, for putting me here, in prison, so I could accomplish what is now being done."

The words shivered through him now. His father, grateful to be in prison with his son. His eyes burned, remnants of the song sung at the funeral rising up to sit in his soul.

The Lord has promised good to me, his word my hope secures; He will my shield and portion be as long as life endures.

He pressed a hand to his chest. *Please, God, help me to believe that.*

Footsteps, and he looked up. Not Rio, not the sheriff, not even Mills.

A man dressed in green canvas pants, a black jacket, with long brown hair, a scruff of beard, a grim set to his mouth strode up to the cage.

Crew got to his feet. "Tristan?"

The undercover DEA informant had been his cohort in quiet surveillance for the better part of a year inside the Sons of Revolution. "Where have you been?"

Tristan ignored him as he worked the lock,

a traditional deadbolt, then drew it back and opened the door. "Let's go."

"What's happening?"

"What do you think? Listen, Mills is out looking into the report of a domestic disturbance—"

"I'd like to domestically disturb him," Crew said as he walked out of the cell.

Tristan grinned. "Yeah, that's what Rio said when he called me. He talked Sheriff Starr into heading up to the compound with Vince and Hammer."

"Like Viper is going to let them walk in, hand over Jo?" He pushed through the back door of the jail, into the fading sunlight. "Viper is on the Ten Most Wanted list."

Tristan gave him a look.

"Where have you been?"

"Laying low. Digging into the financial dealings of the SOR with Jamie. Seems like they're pretty well-funded."

"Like what kind of funding?"

"Like some foreign player."

"You think a foreign government is behind the SOR? Like Russia? Or China?"

"I think China is behind everything." Tristan had parked a pickup behind the jail, and now Crew got into the passenger seat. "But whoever they are, they can't directly source the SOR. They'd need a middleman. Or maybe it's just someone who aligns with the SOR agenda."

"Destroy America?"

Tristan pulled out. "Maybe just break down the will of the people, centralize power. And it starts with money. That's what Jamie and I have been hunting." He had pulled out onto the highway. "You sure you're ready to go back?"

"I'm ready to get JoJo and end this."

Tristan nodded, a muscle pulling in his jaw as he drove.

Crew looked out the window and prayed. *Please, God, keep her alive.* Because if Sheriff Starr and Rio showed up, a showdown could ignite, and suddenly the entire thing could turn into Waco.

And people—most importantly JoJo—could die.

"Must go faster," he said to Tristan, who nodded.

He cut off the highway south of the compound. "Where are you going?"

"Found a back way in a few months ago, before they moved." He had to slow on the rutted road, and then he turned onto an even tighter fire road.

Crew braced his foot on the floorboard, held to the door handle as the truck jerked and bumped.

They pulled up to a fire tower. Tristan got out. "Climb up. You'll get a view of the compound."

Crew had already done the math. He climbed the ladder, coming out on the viewing platform.

Smoke plumed from the camp.

Tristan climbed up behind him. "Is the camp on fire?"

The question hit Crew like a punch. No— no—

Tristan held up a pair of field glasses. "No. It looks like just one cabin, although it's pretty hot." He handed over the glasses to Crew.

He scanned the compound, spotted the fire. The smoke rose, a mix of gray and black, some white. "They're killing the fire." He scanned the other building.

Stopped.

Steadied on the figure hunkered down on the roof of a nearby cabin. "I see her. She's on the roof of the old storage cabin." He handed the glasses over to Tristan. "We need to get in there before they find her."

Tristan nodded but kept staring at the compound.

"What do you see?" Crew asked.

"No sign of Rio and the sheriff."

"It doesn't matter. I have a plan." Crew headed for the ladder.

Tristan came down beside him, hit the ground, glanced at him. "I'm not going to like this, am I?"

Crew opened the door. "You get JoJo. I'll make sure you don't get caught."

Tristan's mouth tightened around the edges, but he nodded, maybe thinking of his own sister, captured by the SOR.

He'd sacrificed his cover to get her out alive.

Sacrifices had to be made.

"Okay, I'll drop you off just outside the compound. There's a gate near the armory. I'll go in there and take her out the back. What are you going to do—walk in and challenge Viper to a duel?"

He looked at Tristan, and for some reason the idea just took hold.

One way to get the compound to pay attention—give the pack a fight for alpha control.

"He'll kill you."

"Maybe not, if I kill him first."

Tristan glanced at him. Then again, Tristan was the guy who'd killed the former SOR leader, helping his sister escape, not to mention he'd been captured and shot by a guy in league with the SOR. So yeah, he got it.

"Better if he stays alive so we can get some answers out of him." Tristan braked, the compound a hundred yards away through the forest. "But I'd prefer if you win."

Crew reached for the door, glanced back. "Thanks for springing me."

"I had a favor to repay. Stay alive."

"Get my girl."

Tristan raised an eyebrow, but Crew shut the door. Then he turned and took off through the forest on the trail that led to the front gate.

Dogs barked, and he slowed. A guard holding an AR-15 stood at the gate, half watching the chaos inside. He turned when he spotted Crew, and Crew lifted his arms. "Hey, Tank. It's just me."

Tank hesitated, glanced at the fire, back to Crew. "Where've you been?"

"Getting information for Viper. What's going on?" He lowered his hands.

"Not sure. A cabin is on fire."

He stopped next to Tank, shoved his hands into his pockets. "You see them bring in anyone?"

Tank frowned, shook his head. "No. Viper came back a few hours ago, but it's been quiet, except for when that chopper left earlier."

He glanced at the guy. Early twenties, a grimy handkerchief around his snarled long brown hair, wearing green camo like he might be in a *Rambo* remake. A kid, really, although Crew might only be a few years older.

He felt ancient.

"The chopper left with all of them?"

"Yeah. Including the doc."

"Okay, well, I'd better see if I can help."

Tank opened the gate, and Crew took a breath. Here went nothing.

The cabin smoldered, gray smoke still tufting off it, but someone had grabbed a hose and sprayed down the building, now charred and smoldering, and if he hadn't spotted JoJo on the roof, he might not have been upright. He refused to look in her direction.

He needed to get the attention away from the cabin, let Tristan sneak into the back—

A couple of the German shepherds ran up to him, barking, but they knew him. Even war dogs could be sweet with people they knew, and now they nudged him. He scratched their ears. "Hey, boys."

Didn't look up as he heard his name, lifted over the fire and the shouting.

"Hey, Titan. Sarge. Good boys. Try not to

wreck this for us, huh?" he said, and lifted his head when Viper called his name again.

The man walked out into the yard, sooty, his face blackened, his eyes reddened. He spat on the ground. "What are you doing back here, Crew?"

Crew came toward him, stopped twenty feet away. "What do you mean?"

Hurry, Tristan.

"We saw you on the camera outside the greenhouse."

The voice came from the side, and he glanced over, seeing Jer charging at him. "We know you're FBI."

"What? No, I'm not." He backed up then because Jer charged. Took a swing at him.

Crew ducked, and Jer twisted, falling off balance.

Crew danced away. "I don't know what you're thinking, but I'm not an FBI agent." Stick to truth. "My girlfriend found the greenhouse, thought it might be weed." He laughed, keeping Viper in his peripheral vision.

"You burned the barn," Viper said, his voice low, a bit of a growl to it.

Jer found his feet, rounded on Crew.

Stay light on your feet, son. Control your distance and angle of attack.

His dad's voice, and he dodged another swing from Jer, who fell.

The dogs had alerted, barking. Sarge nipped at Jer. He kicked at the dog, who landed on his snout, and Sarge yelped, then rounded, snarling.

Jer got up, and Sarge nipped at him again. "Stupid dog." He swung at the dog, missed him. Landed on his knees.

And Crew should have kept his eye on Viper. He knew better, really—the punch hit him so hard it spun him around and landed him on the ground, hands and knees.

He rolled before Viper could land his kick, sprang to his feet.

His head swam, blood dripped from his mouth. But he found his stance.

Remember, balance is key. Hands up, protect that chin.

He held up his fists, eyes on Viper.

The man danced back, almost grinning. Crew spotted a few of the other SORs leaving the fire, gathering in.

"C'mon, Viper, you can do better than that!"

Viper smiled, advanced.

Throw a jab, then bob. Throw a cross, then weave. Make it smooth. Don't telegraph your punches.

Viper sent out a fist, and Crew ducked, then landed a jab on his chin.

The man was steel. He barely moved, shook it off. Got a fist into Crew's ribs.

Crew rolled away, blew it off, and rounded, ducking the cross. Found purchase in the belly of the bear.

A small umph.

Remember, it's as much about when you hit as it is about how hard you hit.

Oops, he'd gotten in too close. Viper grabbed his shirt and sent his knee into his chin.

Crew jerked back, fell onto his backside, blinking away darkness. But he kept moving, rolling, finding his feet.

Every good defense sets up your offense. You have to think like a chess player—always two steps ahead.

Yeah, well, from his recollection, he'd never beaten the old man at chess.

Viper stood, spat, not even bloodied. "This is going to be fun, kid. Real fun."

Crew dripped blood from his mouth, his entire body on fire.

His only move was buying time.

Because no way, no how, was he going to come out of this alive.

Hurry, Tristan.

TWELVE

SPARKS HAD LANDED ON THE ROOF. Some of them even caught fire, and JoJo had debated swatting them out, but that would only attract attention.

So maybe she hadn't heard God correctly about climbing onto the roof.

But that was before Crew walked back into the yard.

JoJo lay, unable to move, a scream blocking her breathing as she watched Crew stand back up.

Viper's first blindside blow had nearly made her retch, seeing Crew practically leave his feet, come up with his mouth bleeding.

Oh, he was tough. Because he faced Viper, so much fierceness on his face, in his eyes, it seemed he might be lit from the inside. Powered maybe by truth, or fury—

Or love.

What?

But of course, his words filled her head. *They mess with you, they mess with me.*

And she'd had to go and make the snarky comment about him fighting the entire compound for her honor.

She wanted to bury her head in her arms and weep.

Especially when Viper hit him again—although Crew had gotten a couple jabs in—and then kicked him across the face.

She had to go down there. Stop this.

And then what? Crew got to watch while Viper beat her too? Killed her?

He was doing this for her . . . so she could get away.

Get. away.

Crew got up, circled Viper, dodged another punch, landed one, ducked, dodged.

The men had formed a circle around them, and one of them pushed Crew back into the center just in time for Viper to hit him again.

She couldn't watch. But she couldn't waste his diversion either.

She backed away from the edge of the roof. Turned.

A man stood there, and she nearly screamed. Long brown hair, a baseball cap—

Wait. "Tristan?" She hissed it, barely above a whisper.

"Let's go," he said, and disappeared below the edge.

Oh. And now, even if she'd doubted it before, she knew . . .

Crew had walked right back into the yard for her. To challenge Viper to a fight, keep the eyes off her.

So she could get away.

Her eyes slicked even as she scooted over the edge, found the window, then Tristan's hand on her foot, directing her down to the firewood bin.

She landed on the ground behind him, the fire still fighting for life in the cabin. But it spilled out enough smoke to obscure them, maybe.

"We can't leave without Crew."

"That's exactly what we're going to do. Believe me, I know what it's like to be left behind, but I made a promise, Jo. C'mon."

No. No. But she pressed a hand over her mouth to follow him.

A glance between the buildings showed Crew

still on his feet, still circling, some of the guys yelling, swearing.

"Jo—now!"

She turned, and Tristan stood behind the cabin, gesturing.

Right. Okay. Maybe she could call Rio, get some help.

She stumbled after him as they ran behind the cabin, over to the Quonset hut. She spotted a metal gate, unseen from her position on the roof or behind the cabin. Yeah, that might have been a better choice.

Tristan reached it, held it open. Gestured with his hand—

A gunshot and a bullet pinged off the metal bar.

She ducked, turned.

Jer held a handgun, walking toward them, blood on his arm and face.

"Get back!" Tristan said and leaped toward her, slamming her back against the Quonset hut. Another gunshot broke the air, and with it now, shouts.

"Run!" Tristan pushed her back toward the cabin, along the fencing. "Out the front!"

She turned and headed back into the smoke and flames, sprinting.

More shouts, and she looked over to see the crowd had dispersed even as Viper and Crew still fought, circling each other. A couple guys had peeled away from them, heading toward the cabin.

"Keep going!" Tristan at her back, pushing, and she stumbled. He pulled her up, and she found herself, got her legs under her.

They passed the storage shed, then a discarded school bus, and Tristan grabbed her arm, yanked her back just as she was about to fly into the yard. He breathed hard, fast, and only then did she see the gun in his grip.

"Just—" He swallowed, his eyes a little wide, and bobbed his head out, past the bus, as if checking the yard.

Her too.

Nearly screamed. Viper had tackled Crew, now hit him, even as Crew wrestled, getting his leg up, kneeing the man.

Viper spilled over his head, but when Crew rolled over, the guy grabbed his leg, pulled him down. Landed on him.

Shoved his face into the ground.

"He's going to kill him."

Tristan leveled the gun at the two, breathing.

"Don't. miss!" She clamped her hands over her mouth, fighting the scream.

Another shot, this time at the bus, and it pinged as Tristan jerked back.

The sky rumbled. Maybe she simply had been too busy to hear it, but just then, right then—

Water poured down from the heavens. A deluge that flooded the camp, pounding down upon the yard, the fiery cabin, the chaos. She hit the ground, rolled under the bus, and Tristan followed her.

The water pelted the earth, and for a second, everything stopped.

Then shouts at the gate, and she scooted out from under the bus to see a handful of men enter, shouting, holding guns.

Wait—Vince? And Hammer? And with them, Rio and men in uniform—looked like local sheriff's deputies.

Tristan grabbed her up and pulled her out. "Go."

"Not without—"

"Jo!"

She whirled around and spotted him, running right at her, full out, even as Rio and his cavalry took down Viper. Hammer had the man in his beefy grasp, a knee on his shoulder, Rio cuffing him.

In the chaos, the Sons of Revolution fled.

But all she cared about was Crew, the way he grabbed her, pulled her up, crushing her to himself, his body soaked through. "Are you okay? Please tell me you're okay!"

She clung to him, her arms around his neck, her legs around his waist, and maybe he wasn't as hurt as he looked because he just held on to her, holding her up.

"I'm okay." Her voice broke. "I'm okay." Then she pushed away, met his eyes. Water dripped from his hair, down his face, mixed with the blood on his mouth, a cut on his cheek. But his eyes drilled into hers, as if testing her words.

She swallowed, nodded, and shook her head. "But you're—you're—oh, I thought . . ." She bit back a moan. "I thought he was going to kill you." She shuddered then and clung to him again.

"All that matters is you, Jo. I'm fine." Although, his voice sounded strained, and she suddenly thought about ribs and internal bleeding and, oh—

"Put me down."

He slowly let her down, her feet on the ground,

his arms around her, a bulwark in the chaos around them.

ATVs fleeing the yard, a few trucks motoring away, dogs barking, the law enforcement securing as many as they could.

She wiped her face, shaken, the adrenaline still hot inside her. "What just happened? I don't— what are Vince and Hammer doing here?"

"Turns out they're ex-military or something." He turned her away from the mess, walked her back around the bus.

Tristan came running over. "You okay, man?"

Crew held up a fist, and Tristan bumped it.

Whatever. "You two are in this together?"

"We had a mission to complete. Vince is down but not dead. Good job there, Rocky."

Crew smiled. Through all the blood, and a clearly impending black eye and broken ribs and whatever other trauma, he smiled.

And then she spotted Skye and Tucker coming in through the front gate.

"The team is here?"

"That's Skye's doing." This from Rio, who'd come running up. "She called in the airstrike when we spotted the fire. You okay?"

She nodded.

"What took you so long?" Crew said, his tone

a little sharp. "And you'd better get those charges dropped."

"Deke's taking care of it."

"What charges?" Jo asked.

"We got lost," Rio said. "I forgot where you said, and if it weren't for the fire . . . anyway, I called Skye, she got the fire on radar and called in the drop. I had to wait until we had backup. I think Tucker sent in the team, just in case."

He turned to Crew. "Good job setting that fire."

"I didn't set the fire," Crew said.

"That would be me," said Jo. "Sorry."

Rio had already started to back away toward where Skye stood. "Good thinking. We would have never found you without it." He turned and ran to his wife.

"Smart," said Crew.

"Desperate." She looked at him. "I . . . can't believe you came for me."

He just looked at her. "Babe. That's what boyfriends do." Then he winked.

And she just couldn't stop herself. "I'm taking you to the hospital. And then I'm kissing you."

"Maybe not in that order," he said.

She raised an eyebrow.

"Could get complicated, since I'm a fugitive."

"What?"

"No you're not, son."

She turned, and the sheriff had come up. Behind him, the sheriff's deputies had the SOR militia members they'd captured on the ground. Viper sat on the tailgate of a truck, bloody, angry.

She didn't see Jer.

"Who do you think gave Tristan the keys?" He stuck out his hand. "I'll get it sorted with Mills. I just needed a hot minute to figure out how this would all go down." He nodded to Crew's injuries. "I think you need to listen to your girlfriend and head over to the Copper Mountain clinic. Then stop by my office and give me a statement." He glanced over at Viper. "And collect the reward for bringing in one of America's most wanted."

"Reward?"

The sheriff grinned. "Maybe I could even put in a word with the governor. See if we can't get you that pardon." He put a hand on Crew's shoulder, then pulled it away. "You're really wet."

Crew laughed, and JoJo slid her hand into his, tightened her grip. "Yes, listen to your girlfriend. Let's get you cleaned up. And then I think you owe me the rest of our pizza date."

He pulled her against him, then slung his arm around her. "Aw, you just want to kiss me."

She looked up at him. "Yes. Yes, I do."

The sky was on fire. Glorious and bold over the western horizon, turning Denali purple, the sun bled out orange and red across the sky.

Crew sat in the ER bay, shirt off, in his pants, as the intern ran physical therapy tape around his ribs. "No breaks according to the X-ray, but go easy—there is a lot of bruising. I'd hate to see the other guy." He looked up and smiled. He wore a nametag. Darren.

"No, you wouldn't." Crew glanced at him. "It wasn't that kind of fight."

He frowned, but Crew looked away, back to the view. *The Lord is good and his love endures forever; his faithfulness continues through all generations.*

Crew didn't know why that verse came into his head, sat there, but it traveled to his heart, gave a squeeze.

Yeah, he recognized his father's voice, weak and near the end of his time on earth, when Crew had visited him at the prison hospital.

Crew had stood by his bed, his father sallow and failing, and the old man had reached out, grabbed his hand and squeezed it. *Have you not known? Have you not heard? The Lord is the everlasting God, the Creator of the ends of the earth. He does not faint or grow weary; His understanding is unsearchable, Crew. Do not be afraid. The Lord will keep you from all harm—He will watch over your life, the Lord will watch over your coming and going both now and forevermore.*

Yes. He'd forgotten that.

At least, until Jo had walked into his life, bringing the sunshine, reminding him of grace and mercy.

A siren sounded outside, an ambulance pulling up. The intern got up. "We're short-staffed today. You good to go?"

"Thanks," Crew said, and the intern stepped out.

He reached for his shirt, sitting on a nearby chair. Winced.

"What are you doing?" JoJo's voice preceded her as she walked into the bay carrying a glass of water. She handed it to him and picked up the shirt. She'd been checked over too, and a terrible bruise darkened her jawline.

But she was alive. And Viper was in custody.

And it was over.

"Trying to get dressed?"

She stepped back, looked at the tape, grimaced.

"What?"

"You sure the X-rays came out clear?"

"I'm fine." He drank the water, and then his stomach growled.

"Sounds like there might be an animal in there." She held open his shirt. He slid one arm in, then the other, and then she put the shirt over his head and tugged it down.

He took the opportunity to grab onto her belt loops, both hands.

"I see how it is," she said, smiling.

But as she pulled the shirt down, her hand ran over his tape, and horror flashed in her eyes.

"You saw the fight."

"Yes." She shook her head. "He really walloped you."

His mouth tightened, and he nodded. "But Tristan had to find you, so . . ."

Her eyes widened. "Wait, are you saying—"

"I'm saying that you're worth the fight. That people mess with you, they mess with me." He touched her cheek, his thumb caressing her face. "What was that about two are better than one?"

She touched his hand. "And a cord of three is not easily broken."

Yes. "I'd sort of forgotten what hope felt like. And then you broke in, and you reminded me that truth shines in the darkness, and the darkness can't overcome it."

"And you reminded me that God is bigger than my fears. He will not betray me."

"Neither will I," he said and ran his hand behind her neck, tugging her down, lifting his face—

Her phone buzzed in her pocket. She'd found it in Viper's truck.

"Hold that thought," she said and pulled it out. "Mom." She looked at Crew and pointed down the hall.

He nodded and she stepped out of the room.

His hand went to his side. The burning sensation suggested he had a broken rib or two, despite the X-rays. Nothing he wouldn't survive, because he'd escaped the SOR alive. And Viper was in custody, and sure, Jer might be on the lam, but they'd find him.

And with Jo's discovery of the larger drone that could deliver the final payload, it was over.

He'd liked the word *pardon* he'd heard from Sheriff Starr. Maybe . . .

What if . . .

He slid off the table.

From nearby, the splash of a utensil tray brightened the room, and suddenly shouts, and Crew pushed back the curtain.

Viper stood in the hallway, a cut over his eye, bleeding down the side of his face. Darren, the male nurse, lay on the floor, bleeding from the mouth.

The zip-tie cuff dangled from one wrist.

Viper looked up at Crew and smiled. "This is convenient."

Crew met his gaze. "Yes, it is."

Viper raised an eyebrow.

Behind him, a nurse backed out of the ER bay, hopefully to find security. No matter.

Viper wasn't going anywhere.

The man rushed Crew, and he saw it, stepped aside and pushed. Viper crashed into an ER table, bounced off, hit the floor.

Popped back up.

Crew found his stance, his father's coaching in his bones. "C'mon, you can do better than that."

Viper wiped the blood from his face, spat. "Come here, boy."

Crew raised an eyebrow but didn't move.

Viper took another run at him, and this time, Crew caught him, sent a knee into his face, rolled, and sent him to the tile floor.

Viper roared, elbowed him off. The hit exploded into Crew's ribs, but Crew rolled again, hit his feet, and hit Viper as he rose.

The man fell back, landed, but Crew didn't advance.

Every time he hits right, he drops his left. Use that.

Thanks, Dad.

Viper got up, his expression lethal. Advanced. Swung, a right hook.

Crew ducked, came up with his own right, the man's guard down. The punch hit Viper on the chin, knocked his head back. He slammed against another table.

Screams now, but Crew shook them off.

Thank You, God, that Jo had gotten that call.

Viper came back at him, another right. Dropped his guard again.

Crew hit him across the face, a solid right hook that rang Viper's bell. Viper stood, dazed a second. Crew could have knocked him over with a kick. But he stepped back, guard up. And smiled. "You didn't really think you beat me in the yard, right? I had to buy time. But I can do this all day, Viper."

Another tip from Dad. Persevere. *Commit your way to the Lord, trust in him and he will do this:*

He will make your righteous reward shine like the dawn, your vindication like the noonday sun.

Funny how the minute he'd started remembering the truth, it'd come flooding back to him, a faucet of light.

Viper spotted a utensil tray and grabbed up a pair scissors. "I can't believe I trusted you. Thought you were one of us."

"I was never one of you."

And that truth simply rushed through, took hold of his bones, and poured light into them.

No, he'd never been a part of the darkness. He'd just let the darkness blind him to that.

"I belong to truth and hope and right."

Viper rushed Crew.

Crew didn't move. Just slapped Viper's hand away, jutted out his foot, and rolled, sending both fists into Viper's back.

Momentum sent Viper to the ground. He howled, jerking, and as Crew backed away, blood pooled under him.

He'd landed on the scissors.

Feet slapped in the hallway, and security burst through the door. Crew held up his hands, stepped back.

Two men, and they fell upon Viper, rolled him

over. He'd stuck himself in the gut, blood pouring through the puncture.

He swore at Crew, but they secured him and got him on a table, zip-tied his hands, then Darren showed up with gauze, and the nurse returned and pulled the curtain.

And Crew stood in the hallway, alone.

No, not alone. "Are you kidding me?"

He turned, and Rio stood there at the door of the ER. "How'd he get free?"

"That's on me." The voice came from the ER bay, and Crew looked over to see Mills holding a cold pack to his nose, blood on his uniform. "I didn't secure him properly. He caused us to crash." He lowered the cold pack.

Yeah, that nose was broken.

"I owe you an apology, Crew," Mills said. He glanced at Rio. "Apparently, you're—"

"One of the good guys."

Crew looked over to see JoJo walking down the hallway, shaking her head. "I leave you for five minutes, and this is what happens?"

He reached out for her, and she walked into his arms. "Then you'd better not leave me."

Then he lowered his head and kissed her. Sweetly, not lingering because, well, he was hungry.

And not just for pizza.

But the last place he wanted to kiss her was in the middle of an ER unit.

He grabbed her hand, glanced at Rio. "I'm done."

Rio nodded. "Thank you."

Huh. Then he took JoJo's hand and led her out into the sunlight.

THIRTEEN

JOJO STILL COULDN'T SHAKE THE image of Crew and Viper fighting, again, from her mind, even as they sat down at Starlight Pizza.

The smells of tomato sauce and baking pies drifted out into the lazy evening, and music played over the speakers attached on the deck, the bench with the live musician empty, his guitar on a stand. Twinkle lights shone despite the light of the day, and a few patrons sat at the yellow-painted picnic tables.

It felt like a date.

Crew held her hand across the table. "You okay?"

She'd come in on the tail end of the fight, paralyzed at the repeat of what had gone down at the compound.

Or . . . not. Because as she'd watched Crew dodge Viper, trip him, land a punch, she realized . . .

He'd taken the beating for her. To give Tristan time to find her. In fact, he'd even said that, but she'd thought he was joking.

Not.

So, no. Not okay at all.

A waitress—same girl as last time, Parker— came up to the table.

Again, Crew ordered a pizza—cheese, pepperoni, green peppers.

He wore a bandage over a cut on his cheek, his eye turning dark, but with the wind running fingers through his dark hair, the short beard, the way he turned to her, a gleam in his brown eyes . . .

Yes. Yes, she was falling in love with this man. And maybe it was risky and filled with what-ifs and vulnerabilities and chaos, but instead of being afraid . . .

Well, her conversation with her mother swept back into her head. *I just needed to hear your voice, honey.*

She'd walked out of the ER to the waiting room and sat on a chair.

"I woke up this morning with this sense that I needed to pray for you. And then I had the sense, right now, I should call you. Is everything okay?"

"I'm fine, Mom. I promise." And sure, maybe she should fill her mother in on the details of the past five days . . .

But perhaps she'd wait until she was sitting across from her in the kitchen of her Montana home so her mother could see that, yes, she was more than just fine.

She was a *girlfriend*.

But she didn't say that to her mother. Not yet. She imagined her mother, standing in her kitchen, her view looking out over Yellowstone, the rising bump of the mountains to the west, the golden, undulating landscape etched by rivers and canyons, cut here and there with tall lodgepole pine and overlooked by an endless blue sky. An older version of JoJo, really, with long brown hair, tanned, lean, strong body from her work outdoors. The original alpha.

Who'd never found another mate. Maybe never would.

"Have there been a lot of fires?" her mother had asked.

"Some. The season isn't over yet though."

"The park is dry. It's altering the migration patterns of the Wapiti Lake pack. I'm going to have to go into the bush for a few days, see if we can locate a couple missing males. I fear the drought has them outside their territory, maybe venturing into Bar N Ranch land. How's your pack—Cleo and Brutus?"

Oh. "They were poisoned by some diseased salmon. I found the pups—two survived."

"Oh, I'm so sorry, that's terrible." A pause. "I'll bet it reminded you of Dakota."

"Yes."

"Things that we love never really die. They live with us, awakened in our memory when we need them."

"Is that how you did it?"

"Did what?"

"Kept going after Dad died. You just imagined him with us?"

"Oh no, honey. Your dad was in my heart, but, well, you were there."

You were there.

"I know. One day at a time, with truth."

"Yes, and you. You. were. there."

Oh.

"It's hard—grief. It feels like getting caught in a wave turning us over and over, and if we can't break free, we just . . . lose our balance, and darkness and confusion take over. You have to fight it with truth. Bring God into the fight. And hold each other up."

She saw a woman run down the hall.

Heard a shout from the ER. Got up. "I think I need to go."

"You sure you're okay?"

"Yes. I promise."

"Remember, you're not alone, JoJo."

No, no she wasn't. "Thanks, Mom."

She'd hung up and then walked into the fight.

Now, Crew's thumb ran over her hand, and a sweet quiet settled between them.

"Your mom okay?"

"Yes. She was just worried about me. She . . . I don't know—she had this feeling she should call me."

He arched an eyebrow.

"What?"

"If you had been in the ER, it probably would have gone down differently."

Oh.

And his meaning hit her.

He looked away, drew in a breath. Turned back. "So, it looks like I'm homeless."

She laughed, and he smiled, and it simply filled her up.

"I think probably the guys could find something for you to do at the fire base."

"Like keep an eye on you?"

Her mouth opened. "I don't need . . ."

He winked. Oh, he was cute, despite all his cuts and bruises, his mouth tweaked up one side.

Okay, maybe she did.

He started to get up, but a hand clamped his shoulder, and she looked up to see Rio sit beside him. He wore a grim look.

"I swear, if you tell me I have to go back undercover—"

"No," Rio said. "It's over."

"Yeah, it is."

"No, I mean the investigation is over."

Skye had come up, now sat beside JoJo. "You okay?"

Jo nodded.

"Good thing you were wearing your tracker ring. We got a fix on you and realized it was coming from the fire on the radar. You set that fire, right? Smart."

"What do you mean the investigation is over?" Crew, his voice a little low but sharp. "We have SOR scattered all over Alaska, and sure, we figured out their immediate plan, but what about the bigger picture? Who's the doc? And the big guy. And what about Jer?"

Rio held up a hand. "I reported the capture of Viper to my boss in Anchorage, and he told me to call off the search for Jer. To shut down the camp, bring in the bioweapon, and file my report."

Even JoJo frowned. "As in case closed?"

"Case closed," Rio said.

Crew was shaking his head, "No, that's not—"

"Calm down, Crew," said Skye. "I have a reporter friend in DC who might be interested in looking into this. Rio might have his hands tied, but that doesn't mean I can't tell a friend . . ."

Crew met Jo's eyes.

Aw, shoot. This wasn't over. So much for washing dishes.

But not today, because right then, their pizza arrived. And then the country singer returned from break and lifted a song into the air, and the night turned sweet and perfect.

And then, because Skye and Rio had offered to drive them back to the base camp, Crew took JoJo's hand and walked her down the street, out to the river, where the low-hanging sun turned it to fire and the air smelled of pine and birch and the wildness of Alaska.

And there, he wrapped her in his arms, pulled

her against himself. "Just for the record, will you be my girlfriend, Wolf Girl?"

She looked up at him, laughed. "I'm still thinking about it."

"No, you're not. You're crazy about me."

She laughed. "Really? How do you know that?"

His gaze landed on her lips. "Because I'm crazy about you. And besides, don't wolves mate for life?"

"What, are we wolves now?"

"Mm-hmm."

She wound her arms around his neck and rose up on her toes. "Then I think you probably need to shut up and kiss me."

He made a noise that sounded very much like a growl.

And then, he did.

THANK YOU

Thank you so much for reading *Burning Secrets*. We hope you enjoyed the story. If you did, would you be willing to do us a favor and leave a review? It doesn't have to be long—just a few words to help other readers know what they're getting. (But no spoilers! We don't want to wreck the fun!) Thank you again for reading!

We'd love to hear from you—not only about this story, but about any characters or stories you'd like to read in the future.

Contact us at www.sunrisepublishing.com/contact.

READ ON FOR MORE FROM

CHASING FIRE:
ALASKA

Gear up for the next Chasing Fire: Alaska romantic suspense thriller, *Burning Truth* by Kelly Underwood.

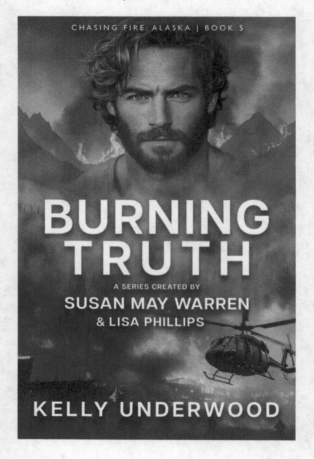

CHASING FIRE: ALASKA | BOOK 5

BURNING TRUTH

A SERIES CREATED BY

SUSAN MAY WARREN
& LISA PHILLIPS

KELLY UNDERWOOD

RESCUE. DANGER. DEVOTION. THIS TIME, THEIR HEARTS ARE ON THE LINE.

She's on a mission to revive her career...

Dani Barlowe, disgraced journalist, has been given one last chance to redeem herself—follow a tip about a secret militia compound in the Alaskan wilderness and get the scoop that will put her back on top. But when her investigation takes a dangerous turn, she finds herself running for her life. Dani's only hope is the rugged hotshot firefighter who comes to her rescue. As danger closes in, she'll have to trust this mountain man with her life...

He'd risk everything to protect his home...

Grizz has one goal: fight fires and protect the Alaskan forests he calls home. But when a reckless, albeit beautiful, reporter trespasses on his territory, he finds himself in the middle of a terrorist plot bent on destroying everything he's got left to care for. It seems he'll have to do the very thing he swore he'd never do again: trust.

Brace yourself for a blazing tale of suspense, courage, and redemption in the untamed Alaskan wild.

REPORTER DANI BARLOWE WASN'T sure which was worse—facing down an actual bear in the wilds of Alaska or duking it out with a pompous, gruff, grouchy hotshot aptly named Grizz.

After this, she was going to change her title to Adventure Reporter, because this was three thousand miles outside of her comfort zone.

She let out a huff that puffed up her blonde bangs. "This trip would have been so much easier if that hotshot crew hadn't thrown us out of their compound." Dani shoved a branch out of her way and trudged forward, her white boots sticking in the mud from the dirt trail. "How much farther is it, anyway?"

Josh Whitlock, the only man brave enough

to volunteer to be her cameraman and videographer on this escapade into the wilderness, trailed behind Dani. "Yeah, they weren't the friendliest. But according to the hand-drawn map your *source* gave you, we need to hike about a mile and a half, right? And are you actually going to tell me who your source is before the case is over?"

Dani ignored the sarcasm-laced comment and took the crinkled paper from Josh. No one could know that a local FBI agent, the husband of a friend of hers, had given a reporter information about an investigation he'd been forced to close.

Why was she sweating under her three layers? Wasn't Alaska supposed to be freezing? But at four p.m., the sun lit the mountain up in bright hues of red and orange with no signs of setting, and her Apple Watch indicated the temperature was sixty degrees.

"My source is one-hundred-percent legit." Skye had passed on the map just last week, explaining that two of her friends, Crew and JoJo, had flown a drone around after trail cameras had spotted unusual militia activity in this area.

They were here.

Wherever here was.

She rotated the map, and Josh chuckled from behind her.

Why were his broken-in boots barely muddy? He didn't have any rips in the sleeves of his company-issued windbreaker from the thorny branches, while her thick International News Network navy jacket looked like it had been shredded by wolves. "We just need to keep going . . . up. Once this muddy trail ends, we should find another pathway that takes us to the secret compound." Dani moved a tree branch out of the way and continued the hike. Josh's exaggerated sigh spurred her forward.

He didn't get her. At forty-six, Josh was fifteen years older than her and on the fast track to early retirement. The man was a perpetual bachelor who loved the comforts of home, while Dani was willing to do whatever it took for the sake of the story. But neither of them was cut out for this little adventure.

Which only made her press on—or up. She wasn't a quitter. There was no turning back now. Her mind had already churned out the sound bites for her special report.

Dangerous militia group hiding in middle-of-nowhere Alaska. Secret laboratory rumored to be tucked into the side of Copper Mountain.

All of it added up to her last shot at reviving her career.

Maybe if she was the one who broke this story

first, the public would forget about the one time she'd had the facts completely wrong.

Her career as an investigative reporter for the International News Network had taken a nose-dive three years ago after she'd botched a story accusing Alaskan senator Geoff Deville of embezzlement. Her intel had been solid, but when the judicial system had found him innocent, the court of public opinion had turned on her like a piranha, shredding her reputation. She'd clawed her way back to the top to regain the trust of viewers. Barely.

No way was she going to give up. Not when she'd come all this way to find a new story.

Not that she'd ever give up on proving Deville wasn't entirely innocent of wrongdoing. The man had a shady past, and if he stepped out of line, Dani would pounce.

She shimmied out of her jacket, tied it around her waist, and marched forward. "I trust my contact. There's a compound or a secret laboratory tucked away in these quiet mountains. I can smell it."

Josh grunted. "That's just how fresh air smells. Something you're not familiar with, living in Washington, DC. When's the last time you even went to a park or did anything outside? What did that hotshot call you?"

Diva Dani.

Why had they stopped at the Midnight Sun base camp first anyway? All she'd wanted to do was connect with her old friend, smokejumper Skye Parker, before following up on the information Skye and her husband, FBI Agent Rio Parker, had sent her. Instead, Dani had ended up facing off with a bunch of cranky hotshots.

One in particular had made her blood boil.

Grizz.

The man certainly resembled a grizzly bear, with his dark-brown shaggy hair, a bushy beard, thick shoulders, and that lumberjack T-shirt with the hotshot logo that stretched across his chest and showed off every one of his rippling muscles.

Get your head in the game, Barlowe.

Something about this thin mountain air had short-circuited her brain.

"Look." Dani turned toward Josh, but her feet wouldn't move. Her designer boots made a sucking sound with each mud-filled step. Josh grabbed her arm to steady her so she could free herself from the guck.

She shook the memories of the hotshots from her mind. If she wanted to come out on top, she had to put in the hard work now. It was up to her to make things happen. No one was showing up to help her save her career. Not her family, friends, or even God. Josh was only here for the overtime. People had showed their true colors the moment Dani's reporter status had soured and she wasn't the media darling anymore.

No. Second place wasn't an option for her.

She shook from Josh's grasp on her arm and trudged forward. "We'll make it there and back before dark, no problem. I've run a marathon before. How hard is a mile-and-a-half hike through the woods?"

Josh snorted. "Not that I want to agree with that hotshot—what was his name? Grizz? But are you sure you're good in those boots?"

She looked down at her once-white fluffy ski boots, now brown and caked with dirt. "Well, I figured if they were good enough for skiing, they'd be fine for Alaska."

What did she know about hiking, or skiing for that matter? She was more of an indoorsy girl. Maybe she should have done better research before booking the first flight out of DC after getting this lead.

Dani tucked fallen strands of her shoulder-length blonde hair back under her multicolor knit cap. "I can't believe you're taking that Neanderthal's side. That guy was the definition of *backwoods*. I can't believe he said we had a death wish. So insufferable. He practically yelled at us."

It almost seemed like Alaskan Mountain Man had gotten under her skin.

No, she wouldn't let that happen. Even if the guy was her type, relationships were just a distraction. She needed to focus on increasing her public approval ratings.

Dani shoved another tree branch out of her way only for it to whip back into her face. Who lived like this?

She looked around and saw nothing but brown and dark-green foliage. No noises except some buzzing insects or an occasional chirping bird. Her apartment in DC had all the modern conveniences a person wanted. But this? They were miles from that general store and restaurant they'd passed on the way up the mountain.

"Admit it, Dani, you're out of your element. There's no shame in us turning around. Especially when your lead is based on a rumor. The government isn't even investigating this claim. Maybe we should just return to the hotshot base and wait for your friend to return."

Without this story, she had nothing left. Her

boss had read her the riot act. *Don't bother returning unless you have the story.*

She tamped down her frustration and kept walking. "Something's going on in these woods, and we're going to be the first to report it."

"Not sure it's worth risking my life."

"You can quit if you want, Josh. Go back and tell stories by the campfire with those hotshots. But I'm going to find out what's happening with this secret lab in the woods. What if it's a terrorist camp? We need to expose it so someone will investigate."

He shook his head. "The hotshots wouldn't give us the time of day. Not after our station roasted them on air. I don't want to face them again."

On the inside, Dani let out a sigh of relief.

She remembered the scathing story her station had run. It'd been a low blow when the hotshots had refused to take them to the location. She should have called ahead to make sure Skye was available this morning. They'd been friends since college, so when Rio's investigation had been stonewalled, he'd had Skye feed her information about this dangerous group in the hope Dani could break the story wide open. Too bad the smokejumpers had been out fighting a fire when she and Josh had arrived. Instead of seeing Skye and letting her know Dani was on the case, they'd been shown the door.

She refused to give up, even if it meant spending the night roughing it on the side of a mountain.

Which was exactly what those hotshots had predicted.

So what if she had a homemade map and zero outdoor survival skills? If she could swim in the Washington, DC fish tank of political piranhas, she could survive a mountain hike.

But hiking a mountain to an undisclosed location in the hopes of breaking a story?

Hold my extra-hot, sugar-free, oat milk latte . . . because this is where Dani Barlowe shines.

She pulled the map from her jacket pocket and studied it. A raindrop plopped on the paper, blurring the ink. She shielded it with her hand.

"Here's where we parked the car, at the entrance to the national park. And I see the end of the nature trail, which means we should find another pathway that takes us up the mountain. We're going to be just fine. You'll see."

As if to mock her, the Alaskan skies opened up, and rain soaked them. She shoved the map into her dry pocket, hoping it would stay protected.

After two and a half hours battling tree limbs, flooding, a deranged beaver, a snake, and an army of mosquitoes, they reached the end of the trail. The dirt path faded into overgrown shrubs and a wall of rocks.

Dani's pulse hammered in her ears. She hadn't come all this way to walk away with nothing. There had to be a second path to follow. So far, the map hadn't gotten them lost. "Look, there's a section of brush that's worn down. I bet this is the way."

Josh gaped at her. "Dani, I have a bad feeling about this."

She put her hands on her hips, her multiple layers of sweaters under her windbreaker making her arms look like the Stay Puft Marshmallow Man. Okay, so maybe she'd overdressed a bit, as indicated by the sweat rolling down her back. "Let's check this path, and if we don't find anything in a half hour, we'll turn around."

He nodded, but his pale face and huffed breath indicated he wasn't fully on board. At least he followed her through the narrow opening that led up. Just . . . up.

The rain intensified, and the trees provided minimal shelter from the deluge. She was soaked four layers deep. *Path* wasn't the correct term for their route. This was the definition of off-grid. No markings or any kind of directional signs. No signs of human life. Just some trampled earth that indicated hikers had at one point headed off the beaten path in this direction. Were they going to find anything on this deserted mountainside? And how long would it take to get back to civilization, anyway?

They trekked on without talking. Her labored breaths rattled around in her ears.

A buzzing sound stopped her dead in her tracks. At her abrupt stop, Josh bumped into her.

"What was that?" Dani whispered. But in the quiet of the mountainside, it sounded like she had a megaphone.

"Sounds man-made. Like electricity."

Her heart beat double time. This was it.

The mystery compound.

They crept through the branches and bushes. Adrenaline fueled Dani's feet, despite the ache in her calves from the mountain hike. She swept a tree limb out of her way and spotted a chain-link fence in the clearing below them, complete with razor-sharp barbed wire across the top.

"Whoa." Josh took his camera out of the bag and began filming. "What is this place?"

They ducked down and watched the valley

below. They were far enough away to not be spotted, but Dani didn't trust that one crackle of a tree branch underfoot wouldn't give away their hiding location.

At least they were higher than the camp and could see directly into it. Behind the fence were several buildings, camouflaged in brown and green colors. One of the huts was three times the size of the others, with what looked like steel doors and solid walls.

"Whatever this is, it can't be good." Josh stood beside her, surveying the scene below. His breath was heavy. From exertion or fear?

Dani couldn't respond. All she could do was take it in.

She'd found her story.

Movement inside the compound caught her attention. Two men in army fatigues came into view with M4 assault rifles slung over their shoulders. They dragged a man through the courtyard and into the middle of the compound.

Even from a distance, Dani could see the gray-haired man stumble, his once-white shirt tattered and stained with . . . blood?

"Get a close-up of their faces." A third man exited the building. "Especially that guy." Something about the man made Dani's insides quake.

He walked with an air of authority and barked orders to the other two men, although she couldn't hear what he was saying. But the man was definitely familiar. She'd examine the footage later.

One of the men opened the door to the main hut and dragged the prisoner inside, but not before Dani got a good look inside. "Josh, did you see that stack of weapons? Did you get a picture of it?" A rack of rocket launchers and guns along one wall.

Josh nodded, his eyes wide. "Who are these men?"

A knot tightened in the pit of Dani's stomach. "They may be part of a rebel group known as the Sons of Revolution. But that's a lot of firepower hidden in the side of a mountain."

She needed to get back to civilization in time to report her findings. With any luck, they could be on the air for the morning East Coast news.

Leaves crunched, and Dani turned to watch Josh back up ten steps, his eyes wide and his hands trembling around the camera. "I can't . . . we shouldn't be here. We've got enough footage. We need to leave."

"Wait. We need to see what's going on. Get more evidence. We need to stick together. Just thirty seconds more—"

Josh set the camera on a rock. "You stay. I'm leaving. With or without you. I'm not risking my life for a story. No job is worth this. Admit it, we're in over our heads."

A chimney puffed out white smoke—more like an industrial smokestack than a cozy fireplace.

A chill raced through Dani, and it wasn't because of the Alaska temperatures. According to Skye, SOR had been testing a biological weapon designed to poison food and water supplies. Fish and other animals in the area had died when exposed to the toxin. Skye's team had helped shut down SOR's base camp, had even destroyed their warehouse along with most of the toxin, but the toxin had to have been made somewhere.

Was that what was going on behind those walls? And why hadn't the FBI shut this group down?

She turned to tell Josh they needed to run in just a few seconds, but he was gone.

All she could hear was the pounding of her heart. There wasn't a person in sight for miles that could help her now that Josh had fled. The discarded camera perched on a stone was the only reminder that he'd been there a few seconds ago.

She looked over the ridge. These men were dangerous, and she was alone. She checked her phone and wanted to toss it down the mountain. No bars. She shoved it into her coat pocket.

How had her laser-focused reporter instincts derailed her so badly? Both Josh and Grizz had tried to warn her, but she hadn't listened.

She'd take Grizz's ornery nature in a heartbeat over her odds with militant men and a secret compound. Her mind went numb, and her hands wouldn't cooperate. Those men hadn't seen her. At least she could still collect evidence for the authorities. And her story that would inevitably follow.

Dani turned on the camera, hit record, and scanned the compound to document everything.

How was she going to get out of the woods? At least she had the map. It was still light outside, and it would be until late, surely. But would she be stuck hiking down the mountain in the dark anyway?

Don't panic. Do. not. panic.

A scream shredded the silence.

Dani froze with the camera rolling. She watched as the guards dragged another prisoner across the courtyard.

Not a prisoner.

The man had a windbreaker on, and Dani

could see the yellow INN logo calling to her like a beacon.

International News Network. Her network. Josh.

What were they going to do to him?

She had to rescue her cameraman. But how? She looked around for a rock to throw or something she could use as a weapon. Maybe she could set off a distraction and give Josh time to run.

But then what? She wouldn't be able to fight these guys off when they inevitably came for her.

No weapons. No self-defense skills. No contact with the outside world.

Her legs gave out and she pitched forward, her knees hitting the dirt. Her breaths came short and fast, and she clutched her chest, willing her lungs to take in air.

The gunshot stopped her heart. Josh slumped to the dirt, and the men behind the fence turned to look at her.

Dani realized then that she'd screamed.

No no no. Adrenaline surged, and her brain shouted for her to run.

She sprinted through the woods, part of her trying to remain quiet while the other part shouted at her to pick up speed.

She tripped and dropped the camera.

No time to retrieve it. She righted herself and raced forward.

Behind her, a twig snapped. At this point, she prayed it was a bear.

Chancing a look over her shoulder, she saw a man through the tree branches. Make that two men. With big guns. She froze, but it didn't matter. They'd spotted her.

She bolted, tree limbs whipping her in the face. The mud from the rain made the terrain slippery, and she prayed her feet wouldn't fly out from under her. Down the mountain she went.

A bullet whizzed by her head. She clamped her mouth shut, but it didn't stop the scream that reverberated across the mountainside.

She was going to die on this mountain. And no one was coming to her rescue.

Grizz glanced at his watch for the third time. This unnecessary delay was cutting into his time off. He was out of here, as soon as Skye finished yelling at the crew.

"I don't care if Dani's station was the one that had that unflattering report about the hotshots. You should have helped her." Skye's voice bounced off the metal walls of the long rectangular building that doubled as their mess hall. He needed to get to the vehicle bay where he'd stashed his ATV. After working and living three months at base camp, Grizz couldn't wait to get back to his cabin.

"I can't believe you sent her away to climb Copper Mountain on her own." Skye glared at Mack, Hammer, Saxon, and Grizz individually. "You know we've had some flash flooding and mudslides from the rain."

This was not his first time being on the receiving end of a dressing down by someone who wasn't his superior. But they'd had it coming.

The Trouble Boys were in trouble. Again. And somehow, Grizz had gotten lumped in with them.

So maybe he could have stepped in and cut the glitzy woman some slack.

Nah.

Far as Grizz was concerned, that diva city reporter had no business hiking Copper Mountain to chase a rumor of a secret compound.

He'd never be able to protect someone so headstrong from the wilds of Alaska. Grizz had hung up his superhero cape long ago.

"In our defense," Mack said, "she didn't tell us she knew you. And you should have seen her outfit. All she needed was one of those teeny purse dogs and she would have rivaled a Kardashian."

Grizz looked to the big man standing next to him. Hammer, Mack's older brother, said nothing, leaving Mack to run his mouth. Saxon flanked the other side of Hammer, not bothering to insert himself in the discussion. Mack was the youngest of the group and had a lot to learn—although anyone under the age of twenty-five was a kid as far as Grizz was concerned. Sometimes it paid to stay quiet.

Three of the hotshots were ex-Army like him, but Grizz had never met Hammer, Saxon, or Kane while he was serving. He didn't know why they'd chosen wildland firefighting or why they'd brought Hammer's kid brother along. But he knew it had something to do with the female hotshot, Sanchez.

Wherever Sanchez was, that was where you could find Kane.

"What even is a Kardashian?" Hammer snickered. The tattoo across the man's thick forearm spelled *Trouble*. They all shared the blame in making snide comments about the fish-out-of-water guests, but no one was going to admit that to Skye.

Skye fixed her fists on her hips and glared at

all of them. "So you let Dani and her cameraman wander into the woods alone?" Her beet-red face conveyed her anger, underscored by her sharp, overenunciated words. They all knew better than to mess with Skye, because no one wanted to tangle with her husband Rio if he caught wind of the situation. The FBI agent was well-connected, and Grizz refused to get on that man's bad side.

Grizz knew he'd been the worst offender. He'd more or less snarled at the beauty queen while the others laughed. "Her station is the one that called us the 'lukewarm shots' last year after we failed to stop a fire from ravaging a fancy new subdivision."

He'd seen that yellow network logo embroidered on her thick blazer, and it'd all rushed back.

But Skye had a valid point.

What could Grizz say to end this conversation? Skye was standing in the way of his time off. "Maybe we could have been more accommodating." Even if playing tour guide to a couple of clueless reporters wasn't in his official job description, he could have behaved better.

"Thanks, Grizz. I appreciate you volunteering to head out and find them."

Wait, what?

Skye wasn't his boss. Why was she giving the orders? He wasn't responsible for these two city slickers that'd wandered into base camp with some half-baked theory.

He bit back a growl. "How do you even know they're lost? I'm going to check on my cabin. We haven't had a night off in months!"

Skye's eyes looked like they might shoot laser beams and fry him where he stood.

"Fine." Grizz bit the words out. "I'll take my ATV and check on Dani and the cameraman. Make sure they're not bear chow."

Time to play nice and not let the surly mountain-man vibe win this round, despite everything within him wanting to retreat to his cabin. Alone.

Where he belonged.

Not that he didn't love his team. The hotshots had his back when putting out wildfires. But in general, he was skeptical of new people. Especially a nosey reporter sniffing out a story. Trust didn't come naturally to him. He'd been burned one too many times to let outsiders in.

It was even the reason he'd stopped going to church. How was he supposed to trust God when God had so many untrustworthy followers? Everyone had an angle to work.

Grizz watched the other hotshots scatter like raindrops. He'd check on the out-of-towners, but he wasn't getting involved in their drama. Not at all.

He grabbed his gear from his bunk room and nodded his goodbyes to his team. He headed to the vehicle bay where he'd stashed one of his prize possessions—a red four-wheeled Raptor two-person ATV. Not that he ever shared his ride, but he loved the way the vehicle ate up the trails with its twenty-one-inch wheels. He cranked the motor and exited the garage only to be greeted with cold rain pelting his face.

Great. Skye was probably right to send him out here, even if it was miserable weather. That city girl and her boyfriend had no business being out in this rain, and it probably was his fault they were out alone.

Even with diminished visibility and slick, muddy ground, Grizz pressed on. He knew this mountain better than anyone. This was practically his backyard. His cabin was ten miles to the west, but for now, he'd head east and up the mountain trail. He hadn't expected the detour, but he had a full tank of gas, so he'd have plenty to make it to the cabin.

What had that reporter been thinking? As a hotshot, it was his job to protect the people who lived on the mountain, and their homes, from wildfires. If there was some rogue secret camp up here, Grizz and his team would have already spotted it.

Over the last few weeks, their smokejumpers had tangled with plenty of militia guys. Logan had rescued Jamie, a civilian, from a militia compound that had been burned by wildfire. The Feds had classified the information about the compound, so it was unlikely that a reporter from DC knew something Grizz's team didn't.

Cadee and Vince had found dead salmon out of season. Orion and Tori had been certain the militia had set up shop somewhere new.

If it was local to the Midnight Sun base, surely they'd know.

Despite the inclement weather, the temperatures were Alaska-perfect at sixty degrees. He wore his hotshot T-shirt and wondered if he should have changed into shorts before leaving.

Rain pelted him in the face as he drove the ATV along the winding paved trail, but he'd take the rain over the dry season that had sparked so many fires.

He laughed at the thought of Dani Barlowe in her puffy network blazer with fourteen layers underneath. Her station's story about the hotshots brought back all kinds of unpleasant memories.

His team had failed to stop a wildfire from taking out a group of homes after it had blazed too close to civilization. No one had cared that the fire had been started by someone carelessly tossing a lit cigarette into the brush. All that'd mattered was that a celebrity's summer home had gone up in smoke along with other overpriced residences in a fancy new subdivision at the base of Copper Mountain. Suddenly the hotshots had been the villains, inept at their jobs.

It was bad enough that his team had failed, but had it needed to become an international scandal? The good guys never could win.

And that horrible nickname the station had imposed on them . . . *lukewarm shots*.

Even if she hadn't written the piece herself, she was guilty by association as far as he was concerned.

After fifteen minutes, Grizz pulled into the state park entrance. The area provided access to several hiking trails that circled Copper Mountain. One lone car sat in the empty parking lot. The same white Subaru Outback that Dani and the cameraman had driven to base camp.

The asphalt trail ended, and the main trail switched to a dirt path. What were these two up to? Had they made it this far? Grizz parked his vehicle up the hill from the parking lot and obscured it in some bushes to protect it from the rain. He pulled out his phone to call Skye with an update. No bars. It wouldn't be the first time a storm had knocked out communications on the mountain.

Grizz made his way to the trailhead. Had Dani made it up these steep hills covered with rocks and mud? He'd definitely underestimated the woman's tenacity if she had.

After thirty minutes, his calf muscles strained with each step. He paused to catch his breath when the dirt trail ended at a scenic photo stop.

Where was Dani?

Despite the rain, Grizz spotted a freshly trampled patch of brush that hadn't been washed away. It wasn't a marked trail, but Grizz had a feeling Dani and the cameraman had continued on, so he set out on foot, up the path beyond where most tourists and locals stopped hiking.

Grizz navigated through the trees and shrubs, climbing the steep slope of the mountain. How far had Dani and her friend hiked? What was so important to her that she'd make this treacherous climb?

He pushed another branch out of his way and froze. A strong, earthy smell hit his nose. The sound of water flowing rumbled close by.

It had the markings of a mudslide. The past few rainy days had taken a toll on the mountain. A few minutes later, Grizz reached the spot where the water, mud, rocks, and debris flowed down the mountainside. It drifted by him and headed toward the road he'd taken in, which meant getting back to base would be treacherous. His ATV wouldn't handle mud in its engine.

He walked parallel to the flow of muck, looking for any signs of Dani and the cameraman.

A boulder interrupted the flow of the mudslide, which sent the river of dirt and debris around it. But Grizz saw the flash of yellow.

The INN logo.

A lifeless figure lay scrunched up against the rock, covered in mud.

He raced to the boulder and stepped through the muck to clear away some of the sludge. "Oh no no no."

Dani lay sprawled in the guck. He checked for breath and found a pulse. Her blonde hair stuck up at odd angles all around her pale face, but she was alive.

"Dani, can you hear me?"

A groan sent his heart soaring, but she didn't rouse. Her pulse was strong, and he didn't see any blood or injuries apart from the knot on her head that swelled beneath his fingers. Her dark-blonde eyelashes lay flat on high cheeks.

What had happened to her? And where was the cameraman?

The rain intensified.

After assessing her injuries, he deemed it safe to move her, so he hoisted her up and cradled her in his arms.

She never woke or even flinched.

Grizz headed back to his ATV, making each step deliberate so as not to slip. His head swiveled on alert, looking for danger but also for the man that had been with Dani. Where was the preppy one with the camera?

And how had she slipped and slid down the mountain in a mudslide?

He looked up the mountainside but didn't see anything alarming.

Then the hair on his arms rose, and Grizz's instincts all went on high alert.

Someone was watching them.

Dani still wasn't moving. Grizz made the decision to get her off the mountain and get help. As he hoisted her up in his arms, he craned his neck around the area. Where was the cameraman? He'd have to go back once he got Dani out of the pelting rain and made sure she was stable.

The mountain was too quiet, other than the trickle from the flowing mud. Grizz marched one foot in front of the other, each step planted firmly to keep from stumbling while carrying Dani.

The sound of a gunshot sent him sprinting down the mountain. Bark exploded from a tree in front of him, sending shards of wood flying.

This wasn't some hunter mistaking him for a caribou. Had Dani stumbled into something?

Grizz doubled his grip on the reporter and zig-zagged his way down the trail, toward the ATV. He thought about taking her rental car but didn't have the keys ... or time. Whoever was at the end of that high-powered rifle might give chase.

Grizz set Dani in the front of his ATV, sand-wiched between him and the handlebars. Her head lolled to the side, and he wrapped his arm around her, letting her fall against his chest.

Not that he'd talked with God much lately, but he sent up a quick prayer that the trail hadn't washed out with the mudslide like he'd antici-pated.

When he got to the narrow trail, it was filled with muck. Dani's SUV was sitting in the equiva-lent of swamp water. No way would her car make it down the only access road to civilization. At least he'd parked his ATV on higher ground.

"Just great." They were cut off from the main way up and down the mountain. Why would he expect God listen to him? Grizz had been radio silent for a long time.

The rain intensified, and Grizz pointed his ATV toward his cabin. A little farther up the mountain, he could pick up another paved trail that led home. He'd just have to off-road it for a bit. At least it would get them out of the rain and away from a shooter. Dani could be dry and warm when she woke up, and he could figure out a way to call for help.

The ATV wheels flicked dirt and mud behind him while his racing mind conjured up scenarios as to what had happened to the other guy—her friend.

After thirty minutes of navigating on and off the trail through the rain, Grizz parked the ATV and killed the motor.

Home sweet home.

He hadn't laid eyes on his cabin in a few months. Plenty of forest fires had kept his team round-the-clock busy.

The cabin lay on five acres of pristine forest nestled in the heart of Copper Mountain. The pine trees acted as a wall all around his cabin, offering protection with their thick branches and foliage.

In the distance, several mountain peaks broke through the horizon. The cabin was Grizz's safe haven in the middle of the untamed, unspoiled wilderness. His nearest neighbor was the perfect distance of two miles away.

His grandfather had built the cabin when Grizz was young and left it to him when he passed away. Once Grizz had returned from serving in the Army, this had been the closest thing he'd had to a home.

With its espresso-colored wood-grain finish and wraparound porch, Grizz's place might not have all the modern amenities like some of the other monstrous summer homes rich people built farther down the mountain, but it was all his, complete with a few personal touches he'd added to the outhouse.

He smiled. Now, that was special—not a functioning outhouse like when his grandparents had lived here, but definitely very useful.

Grizz lifted Dani and carried her into his house—across the threshold, even though he wasn't the marrying kind and she wasn't the kind of woman for him. He couldn't wait to kick off his muddy boots and line them up under the hooks where he kept his winter gear. At home, he could be himself. Kick back, relax, yet still be on high alert.

If that shooter came looking for Dani, Grizz would be ready.

The main room consisted of a living room, complete with wood-burning stove in the right-hand corner, which heated the whole place in the winter, and a kitchen area on the left wall, where his grandmother's mustard-yellow refrigerator rattled and hummed. Probably nothing compared to Dani's expensive tastes. But Grizz took good care of his cabin after inheriting it from his grandparents.

He set her on his grandpa's denim-blue couch, covered her with a fleece blanket, and let out a deep breath. Her presence threw off the vibe of his cabin. Despite his love for his team, he rarely had any visitors to his place.

He strode across the room and tossed the useless phone with no bars on the circle dinette table that overlooked the front window, then sat to unlace his muddy boots.

Should he leave her here and hike to his neighbor? The guy was a medic. He might know how long it would take her to wake up.

But a scream answered his question.

Dani bolted upright, her eyes wild.

He took a step toward her, about to speak, when she screamed again.

"Stay away from me. Help!"

AKNOWLEDGEMENTS

I want to express my heartfelt gratitude to Lisa Phillips, whose incredible talent and creativity not only helped inspire the idea for *Burning Secrets* but also keeps this series alive and thriving. Lisa, your vision and dedication are a constant source of inspiration.

A huge thank you to Katie Donovan, who somehow manages to keep everything organized and running smoothly—without you, we'd be lost in chaos. Your steady hand keeps us on track, and I'm endlessly grateful.

To Sarah Erredge, our brilliant cover designer, thank you for consistently creating covers that make me say, "Wow!" And to Tari Faris, our book designer, thank you for bringing your magic to this series with such beautiful and eye-catching designs.

Rel and Essie, your tireless efforts in promoting

this series do not go unnoticed—thank you for all your hard work and dedication. And finally, to the amazing Sunrise writers, thank you for diving in with passion and giving this series your absolute best. It's an honor to work alongside such talented individuals.

This book, and this series, wouldn't be what it is without all of you. Thank you!

With nearly 2 million books sold, critically acclaimed novelist **Susan May Warren** is the Christy, RITA, and Carol award-winning author of over 100 novels with Tyndale, Barbour, Steeple Hill, and Summerside Press. Known for her compelling plots and unforgettable characters, Susan has written contemporary and historical romances, romantic-suspense, thrillers, rom-com, and Christmas novellas.

With books translated into eight languages, many of her novels have been ECPA and CBA bestsellers, were chosen as Top Picks by Romantic Times, and have won the RWA's Inspirational Reader's Choice contest and the American Christian Fiction Writers Book of the Year award. She's a three-time RITA finalist and an eight-time Christy finalist.

Publishers Weekly has written of her books, "Warren lays bare her characters' human frailties, including fear, grief, and resentment, as openly as she details their virtues of love, devotion, and resiliency. She has crafted an engaging tale of romance, rivalry, and the power of forgiveness." Library Journal adds, "Warren's characters are well-developed and she knows how to create a first rate contemporary romance..."

Susan is also a nationally acclaimed writing coach, teaching at conferences around the nation, and winner of the 2009 American Christian Fiction Writers Mentor of the Year award. She loves to help people launch their writing careers. She is the founder of www.MyBookTherapy.com and www.learnhowtowriteanovel.com, a writing website that helps authors get published and stay published. She is also the author of the popular writing method The Story Equation.

Find excerpts, reviews, and a printable list of her novels at www.susanmaywarren.com and connect with her on social media.

CHASING FIRE:
ALASKA

Dive into an epic series created by

SUSAN MAY WARREN
and LISA PHILLIPS

We solve the problem of what we read next.   Available on Amazon

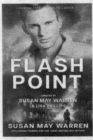

LAST CHANCE
FIRE AND RESCUE

USA Today Bestselling Author

LISA PHILLIPS

with **LAURA CONAWAY, MEGAN BESING** and **MICHELLE SASS ALECKSON**

The men and women of the Last Chance County Fire Department struggle to put a legacy of corruption behind them. They face danger every day on the job as first responders, but the fight to become a family will be their biggest battle yet. When hearts are on the line it's up to each one to trust their skill and lean on their faith to protect the ones they love. Before it all goes down in flames.

sunrise
PUBLISHING

WE THINK YOU'LL ALSO LOVE...

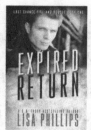

Fire Department liaison Allen Frees may have put his life back together, but getting the truck crew and engine squad to succeed might be his toughest job yet. When a child is nearly kidnapped, Allen steps in to help Pepper Miller keep her niece safe. The one thing he couldn't fix was the love he lost, but he isn't going to let Pepper walk away this time.

Expired Return by Lisa Phillips

Stunt double Vienna Foxcroft's stunt team are the only ones she trusts. Then in walks Sergeant Crew Gatlin and his tough-as-nails military dog, Havoc. When an attack on a film set sends them fleeing into the streets of Turkey, Vienna must face the demons of her past or be devoured by them. And Crew and Havoc will be tested like never before.

Havoc by Ronie Kendig

When an attempt is made on Grey Parker's life and dead bodies begin piling up, suddenly bodyguard Christina Sherman is tasked with keeping both a soldier and his dog safe... and with them, the secrets that could stop a terrorist attack.

Driving Force by Lynette Eason and Kate Angelo

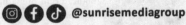
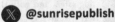
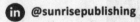